THE PATCHWORK CAT

Other Books by Karen Buck

"Ivy Gets Even"

Killer Quilts Series:

"The Crematory Cat"
"The Saltwater Cat"

THE PATCHWORK CAT

A Novel

Karen Buck

iUniverse, Inc.
New York Lincoln Shanghai

The Patchwork Cat

iUniverse books may be ordered through booksellers or by contacting:

iUniverse
2021 Pine Lake Road, Suite 100
Lincoln, NE 68512
www.iuniverse.com
1-800-Authors (1-800-288-4677)

Because of the dynamic nature of the Internet, any Web addresses or links contained in this book may have changed since publication and may no longer be valid.

This is a work of fiction. All of the characters, names, incidents, organizations, and dialogue in this novel are either the products of the author's imagination or are used fictitiously.

ISBN: 978-0-595-48215-3 (pbk)
ISBN: 978-0-595-60304-6 (ebk)

Printed in the United States of America

The Patchwork Cat is dedicated to my friend Nila Harrah. Her confidence in my writing and her continuing support helped make this book possible. Thank you, Nila!

Author's Note

Like all of the Killer Quilts Series novels, The Patchwork Cat is a work of fiction loosely based on facts or stories I have heard. Many of the places described in the Killer Quilts books are real, but I have taken dramatic liberties and literary license to alter them to suit the story's needs. I don't need to be notified of my "mistakes," for they aren't mistakes.

All peoples' names that are used are entirely fictitious and if they resemble any person living or dead this is purely coincidental.

PROLOGUE

▼

Barbara tied the knot. There, that was the last one. She held it up and cocked her head to one side and then the other, considering her work. This was without any doubt the most interesting quilt she had ever made.

"This will be our ticket to a better life," she said to Homer, who just thumped his tail on the floor in answer. "We can get out of here and start over." She folded the quilt carefully with acid-free paper between the layers, taking care not to make any sharp creases in the cloth. This quilt needed to be carefully preserved.

"Who are you talking to in here?"

Barbara jumped. She thought she had closed her bedroom door but obviously not, her brother stood in the opening staring at her.

"Oh, Sam, you startled me. Nobody, really, just Homer."

The big black lab walked over and leaned against Sam's leg. Sam reached down and scratched the dog's ears. Homer smiled and rolled over on the floor, begging for a belly scratch. Sam stepped into the room and bent to rub the dog's stomach.

Barbara watched her brother make the dog wriggle with joy. She felt a prickle of sweat between her shoulder blades. If Sam had heard her ... but, he must not have, or he'd be asking more questions.

"So, you ready for me to start dinner now?" she said, getting slowly to her feet. Those stiff arthritic hip joints were really singing today.

"Sure," Sam said. "I'm getting hungry."

Barbara went into the bathroom and washed her hands and face. She caught a glimpse of herself in the mirror. She ran the water until it was hot and splashed her face again. There, she had some color back. Sam mustn't suspect a thing, she thought. If he has any idea what my plans are, well, at the least he would horn in on them, but it would be more like him to take the whole thing away from me and leave me out in the cold. He was family, but she still did not trust him. She didn't have a lot of trust left.

"Well," she announced to her reflection, "That is not going to happen." She pushed back her thinning hair and smiled. Soon, soon now, she would have it all. Money, power, and the love of a man who saw beyond her swollen ankles and rolls of fat. Phil loves me for my mind, she thought, smiling. She patted her pocket where his most recent letter full of love and promises nestled.

Soon now, soon.

CHAPTER 1

▼

"Don't look at the clock, don't look, don't look, it just makes it seem longer." I muttered as I pulled my arms through the water and concentrated on stepping as high as I could in my march back and forth the length of the swimming pool. My eyes wandered to the clock anyway and I groaned, only ten minutes of the allotted thirty had passed. I loved working out in the water, it didn't make me ache like dry land exercise did, but the time seemed to creep. Having a fellow water-walker to talk to really made the time fly and I hoped somebody would join me.

Oh, good. Here came relief. I was glad to see Barbara Hughes, a lady in her late 50s I had gotten to know over the last couple of weeks, come through the locker room door and out onto the pool deck. She was new to Stroh's Super Sportz Club and like the rest of us here, determined to shed some of those extra pounds and tone up.

"Hi, Maggie," she said, as she slipped into the pool and churned her way over to me. "How are you today?"

"Not too bad," I told her. "Glad to have a day off, but I wish the weather were nicer."

Barbara nodded. "Yeah, me too. This is too much like Seattle, gray and rainy. I was sure glad to move back to Spokane, even with ..." Her voice trailed off.

"I just came back here from Seattle a year or so ago myself," I said. "Did you live there for very long?"

Barbara paddled silently for a minute. "What did you say? I'm sorry, I was thinking about something. Yes, I was there for quite awhile, almost ten years. The company I worked for had transferred me there, but I got a chance to come back here, so I did, and now I'm retired. Did you live in Seattle for very long yourself?"

"No, not really. Only for a couple of years."

It was funny how exercising in the water seemed to allow for easy conversation with a virtual stranger, almost like going to a therapist, or a hairdresser. Confidences that I didn't even share with my family came right out and others shared their unique stories, too. Somehow, it hadn't felt at all odd to tell Barbara about my marriage to the man who had swept me off my feet and then helped me find my first nursing job in Seattle. He had set us up in a great townhouse in downtown Seattle and she ooohed and aaahed over my description of the views out the windows of the Space Needle, downtown Seattle, Mt. Rainer, and Puget Sound.

She laughed when I told her about Henry and his antics, nothing like black cat stories to make a person smile. She told me she once had a cat much like my fluffy little Cleo and we traded anecdotes like bragging grandparents.

So today it was easy to go with the rest of the story, how my husband changed from a generous, loving man to someone I barely knew. A gambling addiction he managed to keep hidden finally reared its ugly head and ruined everything. I told Barbara how he had gotten us deep into debt and then demanded I hand over the money I had set aside for our retirement. We both had tears in our eyes when I told her how he and a thug named Norm had assaulted me when I could not produce the money quickly enough for them, causing me to miscarry my baby.

"And as if all that were not enough," I told her, "The day after the assault I found out that Phil was embezzling money from Home Improvement, Inc. where he was the head bookkeeper. I divorced him and he went to prison, at the state penitentiary in Walla Walla, last I heard."

Barbara's face paled. "Oh, my, God, that's awful," she said. "I'm so sorry." She looked at the clock and gulped. "Oh, my gosh, look at the time. I better get going. See you later." Barbara hurried away from me out of the pool and into the locker room.

I shook my head, puzzled. She usually did at least a half an hour in the water too, but she had only been there for about fifteen minutes. Oh, well, she must have something else to do today. I finished my workout alone.

CHAPTER 2

▼

I could hear Henry talking as I unlocked my front door. He did not like staying home; he always acted like he was being abandoned, even though he had fluffy, black Cleo, the orange tabby Marmalade, and the big greyhound, Brandy, to keep him company.

There were several killed items scattered about the living room rug, a couple of toilet paper tubes, a receipt, a plastic grocery bag, and here was something new, an empty thread box.

"You goofy guy!" I told him, as I picked up his toys. "I wish I could have seen you carrying around this thread box!"

Henry squinted soft yellow eyes at me, content for the moment to bask quietly in the praise he felt he deserved. Then he came over and sat up like a little black bear, waiting for me to pick him up so he could stick his nose in my ear and purr, loud enough to rattle my brain. I held him for a minute, running my fingers over the swatch of white fur that ran across his shoulder. Until taking a bullet in the skin over that shoulder, his coat was a solid, shiny, black, but the fur in the skinned area grew back a bright white.* Now this stripe gives him a touch of class.

I set him down and he walked away from me, his skinny, rope-like tail held high, just the very tip curved over. His build is that of a Siamese, slim and graceful, with long legs and dainty feet, but I am grateful he did not also have the Siamese voice, that would be very annoying, as talkative as he is.

Brandy gave one soft woof from the kitchen; she needed me to unlatch her dog door so she could go out. It is big enough for a person to crawl through, and even though there isn't a lot of foot traffic that goes by my log house nestled into the foothills of Mt. Spokane, I still feel the need to have things locked up when I am gone.

I unlocked Brandy's door and she dashed out across the deck. She always made a circuit of the whole yard every time she went out, even if she had only been inside for five minutes. There is so much wildlife around that there are always some interesting scents for her to gather. I had seen raccoons, deer, chipmunks, squirrels, and all sorts of birds, but I envied Brandy her nose. I heard coyotes howl in the dark, and even my nose could detect the scent of skunk. I wonder, though, do bears come this far down off the mountain? Or a cougar, maybe? There could be badgers, too. Not to mention all the rodents; squirrels, chipmunks, mice, gophers, voles, and marmots. I am rather glad of the tall chain link fence that surrounds the yard. Much as I like all the wild animals I would rather be kept somewhat apart from them. Not to mention the fact that Brandy would go after any creature that came into "her" yard. Even a big greyhound would make a quick meal for a cougar or a bear.

The cats' door leads into a kennel sort of an area, fenced on all sides and across the top, so I leave their small door open all the time. Cleo and Marmalade were both perched on one of the shelves of their cat castle, watching the birds flitting around the feeders that stood in a row next to the edge of the deck. I am also glad to have this cat enclosure for them. I do not have the heartbreak of chewed bird bodies to contend with this way.

Henry was sitting on the floor looking pathetic. Even though I knew he could easily jump up on the shelf where the food dishes were I gave him a lift. He sat down and began to happily crunch Deli Cat. I pulled my wet towel out of my workout bag and tossed it in the washer and hung my suit up to dry.

"I better get busy, Henry. Rick will be here for dinner tonight."

*The Saltwater Cat

CHAPTER 3

▼

"That was great, Mag," said Rick, pushing himself away from the table. "Want to do that movie now?"

"Sure, just let me put this stuff in the dishwasher first."

"Okay. I'll go get the TV and the DVD player warmed up."

I watched Rick walk away from me, again marveling at his rugged good looks. Gold hair and eyes the blue of glacier ice made him look like a Viking and he is as kind and nice as he is handsome. I looked down at my left hand, where his ring sparkled. Again the question went through my mind, did I trust myself enough to trust him? We had gone through so much, me nearly dying in the process, when I discovered that Lynda, the wife of Rick's business partner, Brad Mancuso, DVM, was using her place at the veterinary clinic, All Animals Hospital and Crematorium, to smuggle illicit drugs. Rick and I worked together for months gathering the proof until we had enough to enlist the aid of the police and the DEA. Finally her crimes were exposed.* After the dust had settled from that encounter, Rick and I discovered we had fallen in love. He had proposed, and I accepted. Now, though, I keep wondering ...

"Hey, you spending the night in the kitchen?"

"Sorry," I said, "I got sidetracked. Be right there."

For the next hour and a half I snuggled happily against Rick's side. The credits rolled and I turned to him, eager for his kiss. His lips had just touched mine when the phone rang, startling us both.

"Perfect," I grumbled. "If it's a telemarketer they'll regret this call," I said, picking up the receiver. I listened for a minute. "Yes, he's here," I said, "Hang on." I held out the phone for him. "It's even worse than that, Rick, it's your service."

He groaned and took the phone from me. "Wouldn't you just know it. Hello? This is Dr. Evans."

I put away the DVD, wondering whose animal was in trouble. But, Rick just listened for a minute, looking puzzled. "Okay," he said, "Thanks."

He disconnected the call, then started to punch in more numbers. "My mother is trying to get a hold of me," he said, turning his wrist to look at his watch. "It'll be the middle of the night in Florida, but she said for me to call …"

"Hi, mom, what's up?" His smile faded and the color drained out of his face as he listened. "Oh, my God," he said, "Yes, I'll be on my way." He dropped the phone and covered his face with his hands, his sobs audible.

*The Crematory Cat

CHAPTER 4

▼

"Rick, Rick, what is it? What's wrong?"

He gulped a breath and let his hands fall into his lap. Tears were running down his cheeks and soaking into his shirt.

"If I can I have to get a plane to Florida tonight," he said, "My dad had a heart attack on the golf course today and died. My mother needs me to come."

I felt my own eyes filling. I remembered how shattering it was when my father died, too young at 47, from a brain hemorrhage. I remembered, too, how much support my mother needed in the weeks following his death. My younger sister, Beth, who was a teenager and still living at home, had borne much of the brunt of it, as I was living in Seattle at that time and I could only manage a few days back in Spokane for the funeral.

"Oh, sweetheart, I am so sorry. What can I do to help?"

Rick took a deep, shuddering breath. He reached into his back pocket and pulled out his wallet and opened it. "Here's my VISA card. Start calling the airlines. See if you can get me a round trip ticket to Tampa, with an open return date. I'll call Jeanne and bring her up to speed with my patients at the clinic. Will you take me to the airport if you can find a flight tonight?"

I was already on hold with the airlines; I nodded. Rick picked up his cell phone and started to tap in numbers.

The next couple of hours were a blur. There was a flight out of Spokane that would get Rick to Chicago by early the next morning, where he would catch a connecting flight to Florida. Jeanne Kasella, the veterinarian who had worked at the clinic with us for only a month, would now have the whole place to run while Rick was gone. She had proven herself as a steady, dependable prospective partner, though, so there was little worry about her being able to handle things. I followed Rick back to his apartment and helped him pack. Almost before I knew it, I was watching his plane take off into the dark star-spangled sky.

Night was well on its way toward morning before I finally tucked myself into bed. I left the skylight blinds open over my bed and watched the stars twinkle until I finally drifted off to sleep with Henry and Cleo both curled up tight against me, one on each side, and Marmalade lying by my feet.

CHAPTER 5

▼

"Are you up for one more stop, Geo?"

My friend Georgia Delman looked at me and sighed. "Okay, I suppose I can do just one more. You're a maniac, Maggie, you know that?"

"Just when I'm in the garage sale mood," I told her. "C'mon, this next one's just around the corner."

Georgia and I piled back into my Blazer. We had spent the day hopping from garage sale to garage sale and were finishing our expedition by hitting all the secondhand and consignment stores in the Hillyard area. It was a perfect fall day for it—warm enough that we didn't need to think about coats and gloves, but not too hot either. We had a pretty good haul of used loot to show for the day.

Our last stop was a big building where people could rent spaces to display their things, rather than having to set up a sale outside their house or in their garage. Everything from new artwork to used household goods was displayed.

"That booth could really be interesting," I said, pointing at a pile of old-looking quilts on a table.

"Just what you need, more quilts," Georgia said with a groan as she heaved herself up from the chair she was test-sitting.

I didn't bother to respond. Every quilter's dream is to find a stash of old quilts, who knew what treasures could be uncovered? I went to the table and started to look through them.

"My sister made all those," said the middle-aged man who was sitting at the table. She never even used most of them; she wanted to save them. For what, I don't know."

"These are beautiful," I told him. "Are you sure you want to sell them?"

"Yeah, I have the one in the house I'm going to keep. I'm going to be moving into a smaller place pretty soon and won't have room for all these. She didn't have any kids or anybody else who would want them, so ..."

These would be perfect to decorate my quilt studio, Killer Quilts. "How much do you want for them?"

"Oh, I don't know," he said. "How's about $10 each?"

I did a rapid count. There were eleven quilts here. That would take a bite out of my checking account, but if need be I could probably sell one or two and make back my investment. Okay, I'd do it.

"How about $100 for all of them?"

He thought for a minute, then nodded. "I guess I can go that," he said.

"Will you take a local check?" I asked.

I helped Georgia tote her treasures into her house. She packed them away in her spare bedroom closet, telling me that she would have to bring them out one at a time, as her husband, Ron, would grumble about the money she spent.

"But, you have income from the salon and your decorating clients don't you?" I asked her. Georgia is a dental hygienist and was working at a dental office when she and Ron met. But Ron had not wanted his wife to work outside their house. Georgia had also gotten education as an esthetician and until they decided to have children, Ron let her set up a small salon in their spare room where she did facials, manicures, and pedicures. She was also an untrained, but superb interior designer and did some freelance interior decorating. Her unique style was starting to catch the eye of the wealthy and with any luck, she would be Spokane's Martha Stewart, only without the prison record.

"Yes, but he still gets grumpy at times," she said. "It's okay. He doesn't notice much around here and if things just gradually show up he probably won't even see them."

"That doesn't sound like a fun way to live, Geo."

She shrugged. "Well, it works for me right now. Thanks for the day, Maggie It was fun. I better go get some dinner started, maybe dab a bit of furniture polish behind my ears so Ron'll think I've been cleaning all day." She laughed. "It's a dirty trick, but it keeps me out of trouble."

I walked back to the Blazer and stood for a minute before getting in, studying Georgia's house. I wondered just how often she got in "trouble" anyway. I hoped my dear friend was safe and happy.

At home I could hardly wait to get the quilts unfolded and spread out so I could get a better look at them. I opened the car bay door on my quilting studio and backed the Blazer into the studio to make it easier to unload them.

I set the box on my big cutting table and started to pull out the quilts. They were of assorted sizes, the smallest being what appeared to be a crib or small child-sized quilt, it was just about 40 by 50 inches in size. The largest ones looked to be queen size. They were in an assortment of standard patterns and my favorite, the Ohio Star, was featured in several. There was a churn dash, and a couple of nine-patch using a unique mix of colors, too.

The smallest quilt, though, was odd. It was the size for a baby or a child, but not in the sorts of colors or design one would usually choose for a little one. It looked like the quilter just grabbed whatever pieces and shapes of fabric were closest and sewed them together in a mish-mash fashion. There did not seem to be any rhyme or reason to the color or pattern selections, either. Normally, a quilt like this would be called a crazy quilt, but this one went beyond crazy and into true madness. I wondered why the quilter had bothered to make it. The top was lumpy with French knots, too. Not a quilt I would want Henry, Marmalade, or Cleo to curl up on for a nap and even less would I want to use it for a human baby. It was even too ugly for a decorative item. I took it in the house and pushed it to the back of the linen closet. I'd decide later what to do with it.

Henry was poking around in the Blazer, occasionally hopping out with some treasure in his mouth, muttering and howling all the while. I never could figure out how he chose what he wanted to carry around and in the time that I had him he had brought me everything from a piece of paper pattern he pulled from the waste basket to a wire coat hanger. How I would love to be able to dive into that little cat brain and figure it out.

Cleo knew a good deal, however. She had already made a nest in one of the nine-patch quilts and was sound asleep.

I spent the rest of the day hanging my new quilts over the exposed beams in the ceiling of my quilt studio. As it worked I thought about Rick. He had been gone almost two weeks now and while I missed him, it was not with the sick longing that I had experienced when Phil and I were first together and he had to be gone. But, maybe that was for the best. After all, my time with Phil certainly had ended on a sour note. But still, I wondered why I wasn't missing Rick more than I was. I heard the phone ring as I positioned the last quilt and I ran to answer it.

CHAPTER 6

▼

"So, I should be home in a day or two, at the most." Rick sounded both exhausted and frustrated. This had to have been a tough trip for him.

"I have missed you, sweetie. How is your mom doing?"

"Not too badly. I miss …" His tone suddenly changed. "I'll let you know for sure what time my flight is and if you could pick me up I'd appreciate it."

Rick had not told me a lot about his parents, just that his mother is a bit of a Southern belle, at least in her eyes. My mother is rather difficult, too, and we had traded several horror stories.

"Your mom is right there, I guess."

"Yes, that's right," Rick said. "Thanks, I'll get back to you with my flight number and arrival time. Good-bye."

"'Bye," was all I could manage before the connection broke.

I put the phone down and went back out to the quilt studio and looked around. Killer Quilts, my quilt studio in the big shop building attached to my log house, looked even better now with the quilts hanging from the beams and in the quilt hangers I had mounted on the walls. The bright colors and patterns made the whole room glow.

Even though I have been here for a couple of years, I am still amazed at my good fortune. After escaping from Seattle, and that's what it had felt like, rather than just a move, I stayed with Georgia while I looked for a house. This log house tucked into the foothills of Mt. Spokane turned out to be perfect. Not only is there this great shop—its wide open floor plan, polished wood floor, and pot bellied stove snuggled into one corner makes it ideal for a quilt studio—but the house holds a surprise, too. Not long after I moved in, I got a call from Eleanor Branson, the previous owner. She told me where I could find a tape recorder with a message from her deceased husband. He led me on a tape-recorded guided tour of the downstairs, which turned out to be a completely self-contained second house. I came to think of it as the panic apartment—a place to go if I am in danger or need to hide.

Larry Branson designed and built the basement living quarters as a safe haven for his family. Not only is the basement fully furnished, including things like towels and sheets, there are even appliances and a phone line that is separate from the one upstairs. It is an amazing space.

The best part, though, is that it cannot be seen from the outside and can only be reached through several stairways hidden in the main house above and one well-hidden passageway in the utility room. Every time I use one of the stairways to go down I feel like Nancy Drew—one of my favorite Nancy Drew books I read as a child was The Hidden Staircase and those I certainly had. There are also secret doors that lead out of the house and into the shop and then out of the shop to the outside, too. Larry's intention was that if the family was ever trapped in almost any part of the house they could escape, or hide from an intruder. He installed a state-of-the-art security system, too.

I told nobody about this refuge, not even Rick. It just seemed like the sort of thing to keep to myself, as least for now. At the time of the tour I couldn't image needing such a place, but within months of going to work at All Animals Hospital and Crematorium, I was glad to have it. A couple of thugs were looking for some of the drugs that had gone astray from what Lynda Mancusco was smuggling through the clinic. The bad guys thought I had taken those drugs and my house was searched and my life threatened. I had come home while they were snooping through my things and I was able to slip into the basement and alert the police without actually confronting the searchers. I hope to never have to use the space for anything like that again, but I am glad to have it.

Now my life is back to normal and I hoped it stays that way. Brad Mancusco sold Rick the veterinary practice and moved to Oregon after all the mess with Lynda and the smuggling was settled. After several months Rick found Jeanne Kasella and once again All Animals has two veterinarians on staff. Few of Brad's clients moved to other vets and it is nice to have a new doctor to help carry the load. Rick and I would be married soon, too. My stomach clenched a little at the thought, did I really want to do that? It had been such a gradual, gentle, involvement; I should trust it. I don't feel an overwhelming passion liked I hoped, but that is okay. Rick is honest and trustworthy. He seems to hold me in a high regard, too, and that is important. I had all the excitement I needed with Phil, I decided.

CHAPTER 7

▼

Pushing aside my nervous thoughts, I decided to make a simple quilt—one that wouldn't tax my spinning brain too much. I hadn't had a chance to do any sewing just for fun for awhile and Georgia had been such a good friend for so long. With fall coming she would appreciate something warm to cuddle up under. I started to pull out fabrics, maybe something with a winter theme would be good.

My back was killing me. Groaning, I straightened up and looked at the clock; no wonder, I had been bent over the cutting table for two hours. I would need a soak in the hot tub tonight, for sure.

But, I did have most of the pieces cut out for Georgia's winter quilt. I found several prints with fairly large pictures of snowmen and other winter scenes on them. I cut out a square from each piece of fabric; twelve squares in all, each one 12 ½ inches by 12 ½ inches. These would finish to twelve-inch squares in the completed quilt, after using a ¼ inch seam allowance to sew them together.

I also had some snowflake fabric in my stash that would make a perfect border. Now all I needed to do was find a solid color I liked for the sashing around the blocks and I would be ready to start sewing.

It took a little digging in my fabric stash, but I finally found a red fabric that really made the little bits of red in the snowmen and winter scene squares pop out. I cut three strips of the red fabric 2 ½ inches wide across the width of the fabric, which was about 42 inches. Then I cut 8 pieces 12 ½ inches long out of the strips. These would be used to make rows of three squares across with the narrow strips of red fabric between the big squares with the winter scenes on them.

I laid out my blocks in four rows of three blocks each in the way I wanted them to look in the finished quilt. I took the first block from the first row and sewed a strip of red to the right hand edge of the block. Next, I took the second block in the row and sewed it to the strip I had just sewn onto the first block. I added a strip of red to the right hand edge of the second block, then sewed the third block on the other side of that strip. Now the first row was done. I made the second, third, and fourth rows the same way, ironing the seam allowances toward the strips of red fabric between the blocks (which is called sashing).

The next step was putting all the strips together. I measured the length of the strips, each one was 40 ½ inches wide. I cut three strips of the red fabric 40 ½ by 2 ½ inches. I sewed one strip to the bottom of the top row of blocks, then sewed the second row of blocks to the other edge of the strip, pinning the strips in place so that the blocks were aligned. I sewed a red strip to the bottom of row two, then added row three of blocks. A red strip went on the bottom of row three, then the fourth row of blocks was sewn on. Then I ironed all the seam allowances toward the red sashing fabric. Next, I measured down the middle of the quilt from top to bottom. This measurement was 54 ½ inches. I cut two strips of red fabric 54 ½ inches by 2 ½ inches and sewed a strip down each side of the assembled blocks and ironed the seam edge out toward the red fabric. Then I measured across the middle of the quilt, from side to side. This measured 44 ½ inches. I cut two pieces of the red 44 ½ by 2 ½ inches and sewed one to the top and one to the bottom of the quilt center. This created a frame around all the blocks. I repeated this process with the snowflake fabric, first measuring the length and cutting strips 58 ½ long and 4 ½ inches wide, then measured the width and cut strips 52 ½ by 4 ½ inches wide and sewed them in place with the seam edges ironed out toward the snowflake fabric as I went along. This made a quilt top 52 ½ inches by 66 ½ inches, the perfect size for curling up in a chair. By the time I was ready for dinner, the quilt top was done. *

*for illustrated instructions on making this quilt see the end of the book

CHAPTER 8

▼

The phone rang, jolting me away from the Spokesman-Review. I looked at the clock, is was just eight o'clock in the morning. It seemed like the phone always rang early on a day when I didn't have to go to the clinic. This is a call I am glad to get, however.

"So, my flight will be in at four your time this afternoon," Rick said. "You can pick me up?"

"Absolutely," I said. "You sound tired. Has it been awful?"

He sighed, "Yes, you cannot imagine. I'll tell you about it when I see you later."

We said good-bye and hung up. Now I had too much time on my hands, and too little. I didn't have enough time to really get involved in anything, but too much to just fritter away.

"What shall I do, Henry?" But, Henry just meowed softly; he was happy napping in the sun that was coming in through the window. "Well, I suppose I could get started quilting Georgia's quilt."

I put my breakfast dishes in the dishwasher and finished reading the paper. Then I went out to the studio. I had already cut out and assembled the piece of red flannel I was going to use for the back of her quilt. It would only take me a few minutes to cut out a piece of batting and pin the three layers together.

My next step would be to secure the quilt onto the longarm quilting machine. There is really nothing fancy about this longarm quilter, it is just a very large sewing machine that sits on wheels on tracks. The tracks and table are about 14 feet long, but the table is only about three feet wide. There is a roller with a canvas strip attached to it on the back edge of the table and another roller with canvas at the front edge. I use corsage pins to fasten one edge of the quilt to the back canvas strip and then I roll the quilt up on the roller. The opposite quilt edge is then pinned to the front roller's canvas. The quilt is then pulled tight, allowing the sewing machine part to be "driven" over the quilt, sewing all the time. All kinds of designs could be done, as the head could be moved in all directions, making curves, going back and forth and up and down. It is much faster than quilting by hand and a machine-quilted piece is very durable, able to withstand machine washing and drying without danger of falling apart. But, with speed also comes danger. It can take days to "un-sew" what had taken minutes to put in. Bitter experience taught me that.

My machine is a Noltings Longarm Quilter. It is called a longarm quilter because the arm of the sewing machine, the part that runs from the head, where the needle is, to the opposite end, where the balance wheel is on a regular machine, is longer and higher than on a home sewing machine. This creates a large opening for the quilt to pass through while it is being sewn. Mine is actually one of the smaller versions, it is about 18 inches from the head to the opposite end. This gives me about that amount of space on a quilt top to sew on before I have to move to a new area. Noltings also made other sizes and has one that is a 30 inch machine. I had seen one, it was huge! Even being tall, I didn't think I would be able to reach across the quilt and sew on the far edge with a machine that big.

I decided to just do a random meandering stitch, called stipling, in the border of Georgia's quilt. Then I would do strings of stars that looked like asterisks in the red sashing around the blocks, mimicking the snowflake pattern in the border fabric. In the big blocks I would quilt around the main picture in each one, not letting any stitching cross the picture. This would make the picture sort of puff out from the rest of the quilt, accenting it.

Like always, I started in the middle of the quilt and worked my from side to side and top to bottom. By two o'clock and with a break for lunch, the quilting was done, even though it had required three changes of thread color and a couple of breaks to wind more bobbins. It only took me another half hour to make the binding and sew it to the edge of the quilt. I made a label and fastened it to the back of the quilt, too. It is so important to mark quilts for those who might own them in the future, at least with the maker's name and the date, if nothing else. The next step would be to cuddle up in a chair and do the last part, the binding.

I would turn the double-fold binding I had sewn to the front edge of the quilt over the raw edge and hand-sew it to the back. This is actually my favorite part of making a quilt, beyond giving it away, that is.

The binding was ready for the hand sewing part. I set it aside and looked at the clock, it is just three o'clock. The airport is only about thirty minutes away; I would get there in plenty of time to meet Rick's plane.

"See you in a little bit, Henry." I picked up my keys and headed out the door. Henry just sent a yellow-eyed squint my way. Drugged by sunshine, he is too lazy to even speak.

CHAPTER 9

▼

I saw Rick before he saw me. His shoulders were drooping and he looked exhausted. This could not have been a pleasant trip for him. He face brightened when he saw me though and I felt a warm glow.

"Man, I'm glad to be home," he said, hugging me so tight I could scarcely breathe. "I'm starved, have you eaten recently? Let's go somewhere and get something, okay?"

"Sure," I said. "Where do you want to go?"

"Let's go up to the China Dragon. I'm dying for some good Asian food."

Rick sighed with delight as the aroma of General Tsao's chicken rose from his plate. He added a scoop of rice to his chicken and dug in. For a few minutes he ate in silence, then he put his fork down and sat back.

"Whew, that is good. But, I better slow down or it's not going to last very long. So, tell me, have things been okay?"

"Yes," I said. "Jeanne felt a bit overwhelmed the first couple of days, the schedule was really full when you left, but she managed to hold on and get everything done. I got pressed into service a lot, took out stitches, gave drugs, soothed the savage beasts as best I could. But, you know I loved doing it. Animals can be so much more appreciative than humans!"

"That's good. I hated going off and leaving you two in the lurch, but ..."

"Don't even think about it. Now, tell me about your dad. What happened?"

Rick took a long pull of his iced tea and sighed. "There's not much more to tell than what you already know. Dad had a heart attack some years ago and the doctors told him the next one would probably be his last, and it was. But, at least he died doing something he loved. Mom is devastated, though."

"I can imagine. I remember how my mom was when my dad died."

Rick nodded. "She's been a real basket case." He cleared his throat. "But, there's even more to it than that. She has also decided that she is going to move back here, so I 'can take care of' her. She is worried about hurricanes, too, although they never seemed to scare her when dad was around."

I looked at Rick for a minute. His blue eyes had lost their warmth and now sat in his face like chips of dry ice. "You don't sound too happy about this," I said.

"Well, I'm not. I have never been able to live up to my mother's expectations before and I can't imagine being able to do so now. She has never approved of anything I did, no matter how well I did it, or anybody I associated with. They were never quite 'good enough' for me. Things could get sticky for you, Maggie."

"You know, she sounds like a carbon copy of my mother," I said. "I don't think I'll have too much trouble; at least her behavior won't be anything I haven't seen before. You done eating? I'd like to go home."

"Yeah. Let's go to your place, okay?"

Rick fell asleep on the way home and he just barely made it into the bedroom and into bed before he was snoring softly. His goodnight kiss promised more to come, but it turned out that's as far as things went. I sat in a chair for a few minutes and watched him sleep, then carefully slid into bed next to him, although I probably could have led a marching band at full volume through the room and he wouldn't have stirred.

We sort of slid into spending many of our nights together. It just seemed natural that if we were at one of our places for the evening that we spent the night there. I liked not having to go home alone, or sending him home alone either. He loved as good as he looked, too, another bonus. I wanted to tell him to just move out of his apartment and into the house with me, but I was finding it hard to make that offer. I wasn't waiting for Rick to prove himself in any way, I was just trying to get myself to trust my own judgment again. I had failed so badly the last time.

Rick was not pushing me; he seemed to feel that my accepting his proposal was the biggest hurdle and he is willing to wait for me to get my act together. Now his mother is coming to town. I wondered what sort of impact that would have on our lives.

CHAPTER 10

▼

The next day at the clinic things soon returned to a more normal chaos. With Rick back I didn't have to worry so much about helping in the back with the animals, although I loved doing that. The best part about things easing up for me at the clinic, though, is that I would be able to get away during the lunch break and do my water workout at Stroh's. This had been very hit-or-miss while Rick was gone and I missed the exercise.

Today the water felt wonderful and I let myself float for a few minutes before I started my routine. I hadn't seen Barbara on the random days I managed to get to the pool, either, and I missed having her to talk to.

By the time I was done Barbara still had not shown up. Oh, well, I thought, maybe she's been busy, too.

On my way out the door I stopped at the desk. Sean was working today and he knows everybody.

"Hey, Sean, has Barbara Hughes been in recently?" I asked him.

"Oh, Maggie, haven't you heard? Barbara passed away a while ago; I don't remember exactly when."

I felt sick. She was a good friend and we shared a lot in the short time we had known each other.

"Oh, no. You're kidding. What happened, do you know?"

"No, I don't. I heard that her brother found her dead in her chair when he came home. Her funeral is next week some time." He pointed over his shoulder at the members' bulletin board. I stepped over to look at it. Yes, there it is: Barbara Hughes, services at Hennessey Funeral Home on North Pines, next Tuesday at one p.m. Rats. That is my day off; I could go. I hate funerals with every cell of my body, but I would go.

When I got back to the clinic I called and ordered flowers sent to Barbara's brother. Her death colored the rest of my afternoon and I was relieved when Rick said nothing about getting together in the evening. He was still tired, I could tell by the bags under his eyes, and I needed some time to myself.

At home I shed a few tears into Georgia's quilt as I finished putting the binding on it. Barbara had been a quilter, too. She seemed upset the last time I talked to her, I remembered. I hoped she was now at peace.

CHAPTER 11

▼

Tuesday came all too soon. I forced myself to put on some decent clothes and go to Barbara's services. Thankfully, they were short. But, the hard part was yet to come.

The funeral announcement included an open invitation to all who knew Barbara to come to a party following the formal service to celebrate her life. This was to be at her brother's place and I was disappointed to see that I would have no trouble finding his house. He lived just south of Sprague on McDonald Road, right behind The Trading Company grocery store where Tidyman's used to be.

When I get to the door of Sam Hughes' house I can hear laughter from inside. Good. This is going to be a party, after all. I take a deep breath and go in.

For all my supposed courage, there is nothing I hate more than going into a room full of strangers and having to talk to them. Assign me to give a speech to a convention center full of people with fifteen minutes' preparation or go into a group of strangers and introduce myself to five of them—which one would I choose? The speech, in a heartbeat. Even if the whole room full of people got up and walked out it would not have felt as difficult as a face-to-face snub. Not that that happened too often, but I did remember one painful incident. At a party I found myself sitting next to a woman I did not know. I said hello and after we exchanged names I asked her what she did. She said she worked for Hospice of Spokane. They do such wonderful work with people who are dealing with end of life issues and I asked her what she did there. She said, "We do counseling and provide medical care to help people deal with death and dying issues." I said, Yes, I knew that's what Hospice did, what did she do, though? She just repeated the same sentence, then turned her back on me, got up and walked away.

Had I missed something? When she said "we" I thought she was telling me what the whole hospice program was all about, she could have been the receptionist for all I knew and that was why I asked her again what she did. I was a bit flummoxed, but I did not try to talk to her again. That happened years ago and I still think about it now and then, wondering and feeling embarrassed and ashamed all over again. Silly, but there it is.

Anyway, that's why I hate having to talk to strangers in that sort of a setting and risking that kind of rejection. That should not matter, coming from a stranger, but it did.

My anxiety was that Barbara's celebration-of-life party could be that same sort of situation.

I slipped in and grabbed a cup of coffee, grateful for something to hang onto, then looked around. Some of the people were pool-mates, I was relieved to see. Them I could talk to. I went over to where Marietta Arnold was standing. I was glad to see she was alone.

"Hi, Marietta. Isn't it too bad?"

"Yes, poor Barbara. I wonder what made her do it."

"Do what? What do you mean?"

"Oh, you don't know?" said Marietta, "Barbara committed suicide."

"She *what?*" I said, stunned. "Are you sure?"

"Yes," she said, "Her brother, Sam, he told me so. That's why it took so long after her death to do her funeral; an autopsy was required, although she did leave a note. He's the guy over there in the green shirt. He actually is looking for you."

I stared at Marietta. "Me? What does he want me for?"

She shrugged. "I have no idea."

"Well, I guess I better go find out."

"Sam? How do you do," I said, holding out my hand to him, "I'm Maggie Jackson, a friend of Barbara's. I am so sorry to hear that she died." Sam looked familiar, where had I seen him before?

"Maggie, I'm glad to meet you. Barbara left letters for people and one of them is for you. I was going to try and find you at Stroh's if you hadn't come today; that's the only address Barbara knew for you."

He fumbled in his pocket for a minute then pulled out an envelope. "Barb used to talk about you a lot. She was so happy to have found another quilter here. She hadn't been back in Spokane for very long and didn't know a lot of people yet."

"We used to talk at the pool all the time," I said. "I wondered where she was when I didn't see her for a few days."

"Barbara suffered from depression for a long time," said Sam. "She lost her fiancé just weeks before their wedding when she was only twenty years old and she never really got over that."

"How awful for her," I said. "She always seemed so happy, though."

"Yes," he said, "She hid her true feelings well."

"So, she never married?" I said.

"No, she never found another guy quite like that first one. It seemed like everybody she met started out okay, but then they turned on her at the end. This last one actually turned out to be some sort of a criminal. She quit her job in Seattle and came here for a fresh start."

I nodded. "I can sympathize. My ex-husband had turned to crime, too. That's why I came back to Spokane myself."

A woman walked up to Sam and threw herself into his arms, "Oh, Sam," she said, "I'm so sorry."

I mouthed a thank you at him and stepped away. The envelope he gave me was fairly thick. I was desperately curious about what was inside. As soon as I politely could, I slipped away.

CHAPTER 12

▼

Once home I started a cup of espresso going in my little machine. I heated up a half a cup of milk in the microwave, too, this would be a latté. I sat down with my foamy cup and opened the envelope Barbara had addressed to me.

Dear Maggie,

First of all, I want you to know that none of this is your fault—I have had problems with depression for a long time. I tried all sorts of medications, but none of them really helped and some of them made it worse.

When I was 20, I was engaged to be married. My fiancé, Gary Miller, was one of the nicest guys you would ever want to know. He worked hard and loved to go fishing, but most of all, he loved me. Just a couple of weeks before we were going to be married he was in a car accident caused by a drunk driver. He was killed instantly.

It took me almost a year to even come out of the house after that happened. I finally went to Spokane Community College and took a course in accounting. I got a job with a company here, then I was transferred to Seattle. After Gary died, I was never able to find another good man. It seemed that most of them were just after one thing and after they got it, they didn't care about me any more.

So, I decided to just have a career. I went to work for a national company, Home Improvement, Inc.

I dropped the letter and gasped, tears running down my face. Poor Barbara. She had worked where Phil Scott worked, too. I wondered if she had known him.

I met Phil when he came to Spokane to help HII set up a new store. I was just finishing nursing school and I told him about how hard it was to find a job here right after graduation, as there are two nursing schools in town. He convinced me to move to Seattle where there were more job opportunities. I did that and ended up working exactly where I wanted to, in critical care in the intensive care unit at Seattle Medical Center.

Phil and I ended up getting married and we had the start of what I thought was going to be a great life. Then, after the discovery of Phil's embezzlement from the company, and his attack on me, resulting in the miscarriage, I divorced him and came home to Spokane to lick my wounds and start over.

My mother was horrified. She told me I should stick by him, that I didn't want a divorce "on my record." My record. Would I have to wear a big red D on my face, ala Hester Prim? Was anybody really keeping track, noting all my failures in a big black book? I couldn't imagine that and my mother's statement perplexed me on both counts, her thinking that I should stay with a man who attacked me and my "record." I shook my head, glad those days were past. I dried my eyes and picked up Barbara's letter. What had she meant about her death not being my fault, anyway?

> I worked in the bookkeeping office there and I met a man, Phil Scott. He was my boss and I thought he was wonderful. After I worked with him for a few years, we became a couple. This was against company rules, he said, so we had to be very careful. We never went anywhere together; I would meet him wherever he told me to. He said he was working on a big business deal that had nothing to do with HII. But, he told me HII would not approve of him moonlighting at another job while he was employed by them and he gave me a large amount of money to keep safe for him. He told me it was all legal, and like a fool, I believed him. When he got arrested for stealing the money from the company he told me he had been set up. He said the money was honestly earned and I still continued to believe him. He said he would only be in jail for a short time and then we would go away together.

Again I let the letter fall from my hands. This is incredible. Phil was seeing this woman the whole time he was romancing and marrying me. What a rat! After being convicted of the embezzlement, he might have just been in jail for a short time, or even gotten out early for good behavior, but his attack on me meant a longer sentence. This poor woman, another victim of Phil Scott. I picked the letter back up and went on reading.

When I met you at the pool it didn't take me very long to figure out that you had been married to Phil, the man I thought was my last hope. Not only was he cheating on me and you, but now I am sure that he indeed did take the money from HII and tricked me into hiding it for him. He wrote me a letter bragging about it and said he was going to send someone to get it for him. I knew then that there would never be a future for me with him—like the others he had just used me.

I wanted you to know that my death is not your fault. It is just that I cannot go on any longer. There will never be happiness for me.

Your friend,
Barbara Hughes

I found myself in tears again and furious for Barbara. Here was another life Phil Scott had destroyed.

CHAPTER 13

▼

I sat for a few minutes and stared out the window, remembering how I felt after my miscarriage. If it hadn't have been for the cats, I might too have taken my life. It was a time that was so painful that it had seemed impossible to go on.

Barbara must have been shattered when she figured out who I was and how Phil had used her. I wished there was some way he could be punished for her suicide and hoped that maybe there is indeed a "permanent record" somewhere and that Phil will eventually get exactly what he deserves.

I got up and wandered out to the quilt studio, not sure what I wanted to do. Rick was busy at work and wouldn't be home until late evening, Georgia's quilt was done and I wasn't really in the mood to start anything else. I looked up at the quilts hanging from the exposed beams, again pleased by how their vibrant colors warmed the space.

Suddenly, an image of Sam, Barbara's brother, popped into my thoughts. He is the man who sold me the box of quilts from the shop in Hillyard. These are Barbara's quilts, I am positive.

I grabbed the one closest to me and pulled it down. I had been in such a hurry to hang them up I hadn't even looked for labels. Not everybody put a label on their quilt, but I always did. A quilt needed that provenance, telling at least who had made it and when it was made.

There was no obvious label on this first quilt, but I looked it over carefully. Some people use distinctive labels, little works of art in themselves, and others just write directly on the back fabric.

Sure enough, this is what Barbara had done. All the way down at the bottom edge, nearly hidden by the binding, I saw feathery writing. "Made by Barbara

Hughes for the guest room, 1976," it said. She had started these quilts as a very young woman. I pulled the other quilts down one by one and they, too, were labeled by her hand for different rooms in a house, all done within a 10-year time span, the last one made in 1986. She had continued her quilting even after her fiancé died. That probably helped her cope with her grief, I know quilting certainly helped me after the miscarriage. She must have made them for her hope chest. How sad, but how lucky I am to have these quilts. Barbara is gone, but her quilts will have a good home for as long as I have them. All thoughts of selling any of them went out of my mind; they will be studio décor only.

I went to my desk and wrote Sam a short note. I wanted him to know that I have his sister's quilts and if he ever regretted selling any of them I would be glad to get them back to him. I went out and put the note in the mailbox then went back in to feed the animals and myself, feeling better than I had all day long.

The weather got colder as the day passed. Even though the house was warm, I still felt chilled to the bone. After I cleaned up my few dinner dishes I decided to go out and soak in the hot tub.

Brandy was sleeping in the living room. The wind was blowing a bit, so I latched her dog door before I went outside. I would let her out again before I went to bed.

I stepped out the sliding doors onto the patio. Standing on the deck looking at me was a large raccoon. They come into the yard in the fall, climbing over the chain-link fence like it was a ladder put there just for them, to eat the apples and seeds that fell off the trees and flowers. I had seen a family of three over the summer, mom and two young ones, who started out small but now were nearly as big as their mother.

This must be the mother. The lights that I turned on didn't seem to bother her and she did not really run away from me, just waddled out into the yard and stopped, facing me. The raccoon had been eating out of Brandy's dry food bowl; I had not picked it up after she was done eating. That is okay. I don't mind treating the raccoons to an occasional snack.

I flipped back the lid on the hot tub and sank into the water, gasping with pleasure. I sat for a minute then turned over to float on my stomach so I could peek out over the edge and watch my raccoon. She stood in the yard for a minute, watching my every move. As soon as she saw that I was settled into one place she slowly made her way to Brandy's food bowl. She sat down on a furry bottom and went back to her meal, never taking her shiny black eyes off me.

The raccoon ate daintily, taking individual pieces of dry food out of the bowl with paws that worked like little hands. She put each piece of food in her mouth and chewed with an open-mouth grimace, black lips peeled back from glistening white teeth. I didn't know how she kept the food from falling out, but she seemed to manage. Brandy's water bowl was right there, too, but the raccoon did not dip the food into it. After the raccoons' first visit I decided to read up on raccoon behavior. I found out that raccoons don't "wash" their food, exactly.

They do a lot of searching in stream and lake bottoms, feeling over the rocks and mud for crawfish and other bits of prey and so they are accustomed to finding food in water. Sterling North wrote a wonderful book about raccoons and he found that his pet raccoon, Rascal, would put his food into water if he could, but Sterling figured out that the raccoon was just feeling the food, not washing it. He discovered this after he handed his raccoon a cube of sugar. The raccoon put the cube in the water to get a good feel for it, and of course, it dissolved. When the raccoon looked annoyed at this, Sterling gave it another cube. This time the raccoon seemed to think about, then did not dip the cube in the water, but ate it dry. Sterling then realized that the raccoon learned that not all food should be placed in water to see what it felt like.

I don't know if my raccoons ever tried dipping the dry dog food in the water bowl, but while I saw them drink, I never saw them putting their feet into the water. The mother raccoon would also very carefully take a dog biscuit from my fingers and never tried to put it in water either, and ate it rather like I would eat a cookie, bite by bite.

While I watched her chew I became aware of rustling noises along the back of the yard by the fence. It sounded like an army was walking through the dry leaves, shuffling their feet as they went. But, I could see nobody. I was pretty sure I knew what I was hearing, though, and within minutes I saw them. It was the kids. One young raccoon is almost as big as its mother, must be the boy, I thought, and the other one is a bit smaller and daintier—I thought of that one as a female. The only way to know for sure would be to turn them over and check out their bottoms, but I didn't think they would take too kindly to that.

The two young raccoons scaled the fence and came over to the food bowl to dine. The larger one started to eat, but when the smaller one tried to put her paw in the bowl I heard a growl. The big kid wasn't letting the little kid have any. She moved away from the bowl and started to nose over the deck, looking for something else to eat. She munched on a couple of peanuts that the squirrels had knocked out of their elevated feeder and some sunflower seeds the birds scattered.

She worked her way all over the deck and in my direction. So far neither of the young raccoons seemed to realize I was there.

The hot tub sits on a concrete pad on the ground and the deck top is elevated above the ground a ways, so the deck top itself is about halfway up the side of the tub. This made it very easy to get in and out, no tall side to step over. This also put me only about twelve inches from the deck top. I watched the little raccoon, who seemed oblivious to me, as she nosed about. She wandered over near the hot tub, right underneath where I floated, then lifted up her front legs to stand up tall on her hind legs and look over the edge of the tub.

For a heartbeat the little raccoon and I were eye to eye. "Hi, 'cooner," I said.

The little raccoon's eyes widened and I could almost hear her thinking, "Oh, SHIT!" She dropped to the deck and her paws spun wildly, fighting for traction so she could run away.

This spooked the other, larger raccoon, and he dove off the edge of the deck just about the same time the smaller one got there. They pushed and shoved madly, trying to cram themselves through a small opening under the deck. They reminded me of a cartoon of two fat men trying to get through a doorway at the same time.

While all this went on, the mother raccoon briefly stopped eating and watched her children. Then, with an almost perceptible shrug of her furry shoulders, she went back to her meal. Silly kids, she seemed to be thinking.

Within seconds, both ringed tails had disappeared from sight. I laughed so hard water splashed over the sides of the tub. Just what I needed, a little raccoon therapy.

CHAPTER 14

▼

"Yes, mother, of course." Rick's voice was loud enough that I could hear him at the reception desk in the clinic. I stood and walked over to his office door in time to see him snap his cell phone shut and slap it down on the desk. "At least she's not tying up the office phone," he said, looking disgusted. "But, now it looks like I'm going to have to take another trip to Florida," he said, pacing back and forth in front of his desk.

"Your mom?" was all I had to ask.

He flung his hands up and flopped into his chair. "She is being totally unreasonable. When I got down there and the funeral stuff was over I hired a company to help her pack up all her stuff and get her ready to move to Spokane. But, now she says that she doesn't like the way they are doing things and that she needs me to come and 'supervise.' I hoped this one time she would be able to take care of her own business, but I guess I was wrong."

"She must be feeling very lost and alone," I said. "I know that my mother has always been very capable of taking care of herself, but when my dad died she went through a really bad patch where she could hardly get herself dressed in the morning."

"Well," he said, "My mother's not that bad, thank goodness. I'm sure she misses my dad, but only as one would mourn the loss of a slave. He pretty much danced to her tune once he retired and they moved to Florida." Rick looked at me for a minute. "I'm sure that sounds awful," he said, "But, wait 'til you meet her." He stood up. "I better go tell Jeanne that I'm going to be gone again."

He read my face well, darn it. It is a good thing I wasn't yearning to be on the World Poker Tour. I wouldn't be able to buff a two-year-old. I was thinking that

Rick's mom was probably heartbroken at the loss of her husband, but, maybe not. I had met others for whom the death of a spouse was more of an annoying inconvenience than a reason to be sad.

My thoughts were interrupted by a scratching, scrabbling, sound. A lady came in the front door with a big gray dog. I recognized Patch, one of our frequent patients. He was pulling so hard on the leash that his feet kept sliding out from under him; he looked like Bambi on a frozen pond. From the sounds his claws are making, it is obvious he is in for a trimming. I am glad for the distraction.

The lights were out in the clinic and it was time to go home at last. Rick came out of an exam room drying his hands on a towel. "Well, that's that. I was able to get a flight out this evening, Maggie. Can you take me to the airport after we grab a quick bite to eat?"

"Yes, of course. What time's your flight? Do we need to hurry?"

"Not really. I don't have to be the airport for a couple of hours. Do you want to go to the Outback Steak House?"

Henry was sitting in his carrier. He knew it was time to go. "Yeah, that sounds good. It's cool enough outside that Henry can just wait for us in the car. You want to drop your truck at home or just leave it here in the lot?"

"Let's run it to my place and I'll get my suitcase. That'll save us a trip back there after we eat." said Rick. "We should have plenty of time to enjoy a bit of the evening, even though it seems all we do recently is put me on planes."

Once again I stood in the Spokane International Airport terminal and watched a big Boeing jet lift off into the black starry sky. I had no idea when Rick would be back and neither did he. But, I had a feeling he would have his mother with him when he got home. Then we'd see what would happen next. I wasn't really looking forward to meeting her after the stories Rick told me. Then I had to chuckle, wondering what would happen if our mothers ever got together. Something along the lines of a nuclear explosion, I imagined.

CHAPTER 15

▼

It was a rain-soaked morning and weather like that always moved me to cook, usually some sort of comfort food that I really didn't need. I just finished stirring up some butterscotch cookie* dough when Brandy's soft "woof" caught my attention. I put the pan of dough in the refrigerator to chill and went to the front of the house. I peeked out the window and saw a Spokane Sheriff's car in the driveway. Headed up the walk was Martin Adams, the deputy who helped Rick and me when we were trying to deal with Lynda Mancusco and her drug smuggling. He also helped me when I was trying to help Amy Sanders, whom I met when I went to teach a quilting class at a seminar on the North Beach peninsula on the west coast of Washington where my aunt Lola lived. **

Amy came to visit her parents, but when she got there she found that they had disappeared from their new home in Seacoast Village, just up the peninsula from Lola's house. Against my better judgment, but because I felt sorry for her and nobody seemed to want to help her, I had gotten involved in Amy's troubles. My hoped-for vacation at the beach turned into a race against death for me, Amy, my aunt Lola, and Henry, who actually got shot by one of the bad guys. I vowed not to put myself in such peril again and now, with Marty showing up at my house I hoped that promise would hold.

"Hi, Marty, what brings you here?" I said with a smile. Marty is such a great guy and I am always glad to see him.

But, this morning he was not smiling and he was wearing his cop face—a look I'd learned to identify when he was involved the drug problem at the clinic. "I need to ask you some questions," he said. "Okay if I come in?"

"Sure, what's up?"

"Do you know a Sam Hughes?" Marty sat down and pulled out a small notebook and a pen. This really is an official call, I thought.

"Yeah, sort of," I said, "I got to know his sister, Barbara, at Stroh's. She just recently passed away and I went to her funeral and I talked to him there."

Marty nodded. "We saw your name in the guest book and found a note you had written to him. Is that the first time you met Sam?"

"No, not exactly. He had a booth at a consignment shop in Hillyard and I bought some quilts from him that his sister made, but I didn't figure that out until later. Why?"

"So that's what that note was about. Where are those quilts now?"

"I have them hanging in the studio. What is this all about, Marty?"

Marty sighed and shook his head. "We got a call from one of Sam's neighbors yesterday. She heard a lot of noise coming from his house. By the time we got there, whatever had gone on was over and Sam was beaten nearly to death."

"What! What happened? Is he okay?"

"No. He died in the ambulance on the way to the hospital. It appeared that somebody was looking for something; his house was completely torn apart."

"Oh, Marty, that's awful. Do you know what they were looking for?"

"I only have a guess and that's why I'm here. The only thing that Sam said that we could understand were the words 'quilt' and 'Maggie.' I figured he was talking about you when I saw your name in the guest book. Of course I know about your quilting and we also had the note you wrote to him."

I felt my insides start to quiver. Had Sam been killed for Barbara's quilts? But, they weren't really special in any way. The patterns were ordinary and some of her color combinations were a bit unusual. Plus, they weren't old enough to qualify as antiques either. What would anybody want with them?

I then had a chilling thought. "Barbara had a dog, Marty. This is a stupid question, but I have to ask. What happened to the dog?"

"The neighbor took him; he's okay. Now, you want to show me those quilts?"

"I'd be glad to show you the quilts, Marty, but maybe there is something else going on." I took a deep breath. I hated having to tell the story again, it made me feel soiled, somehow. "Just a minute. I have something to show you."

I went and got Barbara's letter. While Marty read it I tried to marshal my thoughts. I wanted to tell him about what the letter meant in as few words as possible.

"What does this have to do with Sam's death? And who's this Phil?" Marty asked, putting the letter on the table.

"It's a long story, Marty. Tell you what. I have some cookie dough in the 'fridge and it will take me about two minutes to get it rolled into balls and on the cookie sheets and into the oven. Then, while they bake I will show you Barbara's quilts. We're going to need coffee and munchies if you want to hear my story and the cookies only bake for eight minutes. Do you have the time?"

Marty looked at me with a faint frown. "Yeah, I suppose."

I jumped up and started the oven heating. The coffee pot was still full and hot from my morning dose and by the time I had rolled balls of butterscotch cookie dough out and put them on a baking sheet the oven was hot. I slid the cookies in and set the timer. I glanced at my watch, too.

"Okay, Marty, let's go out into the studio."

He stood up and headed for the front door.

"No, come this way," I said, "It's quicker and it's cold and wet outside besides."

I pushed the button that caused the pantry to slide silently into the kitchen. I had to laugh at the look on Marty's face; I had not shown him this feature of my house.

"Come on through," I said.

"A secret passage?" His eyes were wide as he peered through the opening behind the pantry into the studio. "When did you put this in?"

"It was here when I bought the house. Larry Branson, the guy who built this place, wanted to have an escape route out of the house. There is a hidden door to get out of the studio to the outside, too." And, a whole second house is hidden under our feet, I thought, but I won't tell you about that. I was still getting used to the fact that I could live as comfortably, while not as attractively, in the downstairs as on the main floor if I ever needed to. I hadn't even told Rick about it the whole second living space, complete with appliances and furniture, that Larry Branson built.

"Amazing," Marty said, stepping into the studio. "But a good idea."

"These are the quilts," I said, pointing. "Barbara made them several years ago over about 10 years' time. Sam sold me a whole box of them for $100. At first I was going to try and sell a couple of them on eBay to make that money back, but when I found out they were hers, well, I just decided to keep them as studio decorations. As you can see, they really are nothing special. Let me take them down so you can take a closer look at them."

The stove timer started to ding. I pulled the quilts down and piled them on the cutting table and left Marty sorting through them.

After a few minutes he came back into the kitchen. "I didn't see anything special about those quilts, either, Maggie. Ummmm, those cookies smell wonderful. Are you ready to tell me the story you mentioned?"

I slid a plate of cookies onto the kitchen table and filled a couple of coffee mugs.

"Have a seat, Marty."

I picked up a cookie and turned it over in my hands. Suddenly my stomach was not in the mood. I set it down.

** The Saltwater Cat

* Recipe for Butterscotch Cookies is at the end of the book

CHAPTER 16

▼

"Well, you read in the letter about Phil Scott? I was married to him for a few years and divorced him about three years ago. I took my maiden name back after the divorce; I wanted him totally expunged from my life."

"Wow," said Marty, "This sounds serious."

I nodded, "Yup, it is. Phil was my knight on a white horse, whisking me off to Seattle where after we got married we lived in a great townhouse right in the middle of downtown. He helped me get my first nursing job and we were getting ready to start a family. But, something went terribly wrong somewhere. He either developed a gambling habit, or an old one resurfaced, I never knew. He about bankrupted us, then demanded I give him the money I had put in CDs and an IRA for our retirement. When I couldn't immediately produce the cash, he and another guy, Norm, actually physically assaulted me."

"My, God, Maggie. I had no idea," Marty said, his cop face sliding off into sympathy. "You did press charges, didn't you?"

"Yes, I did, but I really didn't have to. I knew he was coming back to try and get the money and I had called for help. The Seattle police were hiding in the townhouse when Phil and his pal showed up. The police put in tape recorders and got everything Phil and his hired help said. They actually caught Phil and Norm in the midst of the assault and hauled them both away. Plus, Phil was stealing money from Home Improvement, Inc., where he worked, and he was indicted for the embezzlement, too. He and Norm are both in the prison at the state penitentiary in Walla Walla."

Marty shook his head and looked pained. "What a couple of creeps. Were you badly injured?"

Now for the hardest part. "Not really, just a few bumps and bruises. But, I was pregnant and one of them punched me in the belly hard enough that I lost the baby. I told Barbara Hughes, Sam's sister, about all this and I think that is part of why she recently committed suicide. I didn't realize at the time that she had known Phil and had actually been involved with him while he and I were married. Up until a couple of weeks ago I had never told her my husband's name, so she hadn't yet made the connection. When she did, well …"

Marty sat without speaking, chewing at his lower lip. I knew he was struggling with just what to say; I wasn't surprised to see him put his cop face on again.

"What a mess for everybody. So, she was having an affair with this Phil Scott character while you and he were married, right?"

I nodded. "Yeah, and it sounds like probably before we got married, too. Barbara must have figured that out while she and I were trading life stories; funny how being in a swimming pool leads to exchanging stories that way. I feel almost responsible for her death. After she learned about this man who had also wronged her it seemed to be the last straw for her."

Marty stood up. "I don't think you need to blame yourself, Maggie. This Phil would have shown his true colors eventually. In fact, Barbara's life might not have been worth much to him after he got a hold of the money she hid for him anyway. Barbara's hearing about him from you just sped up the eventual conclusion. Okay, that's about it. I don't have any idea what Sam meant when he talked about you and quilts. I didn't see anything interesting about the ones you bought from him."

"Oh, wait, I almost forgot. There's one more," I said, jumping up. "You might as well see that one, too."

The odd little crazy quilt I had left tucked into the back of the linen closet—I still wasn't sure what to do with it. I certainly did not want it hanging in my studio or anywhere else, for that matter; it was too ugly for words. I pulled it out and went back to the kitchen.

"This is one more quilt Barbara made," I said, holding it out for Marty to see.

I tried not to laugh; Marty's face was a study. I couldn't tell if he was staring at the quilt with horrified fascination or true horror.

"What in the world is that thing?" said Marty, staring at Barbara's crib-size quilt. He reached out and fingered the edge.

"It's pretty awful, isn't it?" I said, "I don't know why she made this; the top with all the clashing colors, patterns, and cut-out shapes is odd enough, but then she covered the whole thing with French knots. Rows of knots, with gaps here and there for no design purpose that I can figure out. I have no idea what she was trying to do. I was thinking about putting it down for Brandy to sleep on, but it seems too lumpy even for that. I don't even know why I'm keeping it."

"You're sure that Barbara made this one?"

"Pretty sure. It was in the box with the others. She labeled the others and I really haven't looked for a label on this one, just assumed it was hers. Let's see if she signed this one, too."

It only took me a second to find her handwriting on the back near the binding. "For Phil," it read, "I hope you like it. Barbara."

She had scrawled the words on, not written them neatly like on her bigger quilts. I would bet that she was mad when she made this quilt. "Maybe she made this after she found out about him from me. Now I think I'll keep it after all. Next time one of the animals pukes on the floor I'll clean it up with this and then maybe send it to Phil in prison!"

Marty was laughing, too, and he looked relieved. I was sure he was glad to be off the topic of Phil's treatment of me and my pain over Barbara's death.

"That's not too bad an idea, Maggie. Well, I better get going. Thanks for the cookies. I'll get back to you about Sam, if you're curious."

"Yes, Marty, do let me know. Sam seemed like a nice man."

Marty went out the kitchen door to his car and I sat back down at the table. Now those cookies looked pretty good to me.

CHAPTER 17

▼

I was a little surprised by the phone message left for me the next day at the clinic. "Hi, Maggie, it's me," said Rick's voice. "I didn't want to call you at home last night and wake you up. Mom and I will be heading to Spokane in a few days and hope to get there by next Wednesday. You don't need to pick us up at the airport, though. I have arranged for a rental van and we're going to drive back. Mom is bringing a lot of her things with her and the rest is being shipped. I don't know how long it will take us, but I hope to see you soon."

They are going to drive all the way back and Rick's mom will be living here? What will THAT be like? I looked over at Henry, who was sitting in his usual spot on the counter. He had been keeping an eye on the waiting room; there were four dogs there for their turn with Jeanne and Henry wanted to make sure they behaved themselves. Now, though, he stared at me, eyes narrowed to slits and all the fur stickled up on his spine. Is he worried about the idea of Rick's mom being in Spokane, too?

The front door opened and a red-eyed woman came in, carrying a box like it was full of fragile glassware.

"Muffin passed away last night," she said, fresh tears starting down her cheeks. "It was just like Dr. Rick said, she just went to sleep and didn't wake up this morning. But, it's okay. She had a really good day yesterday, spent most of the time sitting in my bay window watching the birds. She even ate a little dinner. But, I knew the time was close; she crawled into my lap right after dinner didn't get up again until almost midnight." The woman smiled shakily. "My legs were nearly paralyzed by then, but I just couldn't disturb her."

I had to struggle to contain my own tears. I knew what it would be like for me when one of my animals died.

"Now I need to have you cremate her for me," the woman went on. "I picked out an urn last time I was here; you should have that info in the computer. Oh, my name is Fran Miller, by the way."

I tapped on the keyboard. "Yes, Fran, here it is. We will take care of Muffin right away and you can pick up her up on Friday."

Fran handed me a check. "This is what Dr. Rick said it would cost. Is this right?"

"Yes, thank you. See you on Friday."

As soon as Fran left I took the box holding Muffin to the back and slid it into one of the cooler's compartments. Jeanne would be running the crematory later and she would put Muffin's ashes into the urn Fran had chosen and seal it up when the process was complete.

When I first came to work at All Animals Hospital and Crematory it seemed odd to have a wall displaying various cremation ash urns. But, I soon found out how much people liked the idea of being able to cremate their beloved pets. I remembered from my childhood burying our cats' bodies and always wondering if they might eventually be dug up, horrifying someone. This way people could have their pets with them for as long as they wanted or they could scatter the ashes. Besides, the clinic having once been a crematory for humans made it perfect for that aspect of the business.

And, that crematory had saved my life, as well as Henry's, Brad's, and Rick's, too. Henry had managed to trap drug smuggler Lynda Mancuso in the crematory. She had climbed in to remove a rack that was going to be in her way when she stuffed my and Brad's bodies inside. While she was in the chamber, Henry somehow managed to shut the door and turn the crematory on. Lynda was killed. It was a horrid, grisly way to die, but she had been partly responsible for the deaths of hundreds of greyhounds, and who knew how many human lives were destroyed by the junk she was helping smuggle. She was also suspected in the death of the previous receptionist at the clinic. While I would have liked her to have faced justice, I did not regret her death.

I closed the cooler door. At least now I was finally able to come into the back crematory area without getting cold shudders up and down my spine. The time I spent locked in a dog kennel listening to Henry closing the door on Lynda, and then the eventual sounds of the crematory operating, had haunted not just my sleeping hours for many months. Now with Muffin tended to, I went to help Jeanne with the four waiting dogs.

CHAPTER 18

▼

I awoke to an insistent paw poking me in the cheek. "Okay, Henry, I'm up." I stood up and stretched. When I opened the skylight, I saw rain drumming down. Today would be a good day to put the studio back together; I had left all Barbara's quilts piled on the cutting table where I had shown them to Marty.

I poured Deli Cat into Cleo, Henry, and Marmalade's bowls and left them crunching happily. Brandy had her dish outside, under the covered part of the deck. She didn't mind the rain; she ate and then ran out into the yard. With her nose to the ground she followed the fence all the way around in her usual patrol mode. She stopped where the fence met the corner of the shop and barked softly. Probably a skunk or a raccoon came into the yard again, I thought, they did love the gap under the wire at that spot. I filled it in several times but something just kept digging it out, so I finally left it for whatever wanted to use that way into the yard. I wasn't going to stop them, that's for sure. It was too small a spot for Brandy to get out, anyway. Brandy dug at the spot for a minute, then turned to race around the yard and went back to the spot over and over again. Whatever she smelled there sure made her happy.

After I ate I went through the secret pantry door into the studio. I stepped onto the polished wood floor and froze. The studio was a mess. A mess well-beyond the small one I had made when I showed Marty the quilts.

I took a tentative step in and stopped again. I could see there was nobody there, but I could also tell someone certainly had been there. I hurried back into the kitchen and grabbed the phone.

"Oh, Marty, I'm so glad you are in," I said, willing my voice to stop shaking. "Somebody broke into the studio, yesterday while I was at work, I guess. I didn't go in and touch anything. What do you want me to do?"

"There's nobody there now, right?"

"No, at least not that I can tell and I can see pretty well all around the studio."

"Okay," he said, "If you are sure there is nobody there, go ahead and see if there is anything missing. Then call Crime Check and give them a report. Let me know if anything of a significant value is gone. I'll send a car out. I'll be stuck here for a couple of hours more or I'd come myself."

"Thanks, Marty. I'll go walk around the whole studio. From the door I could see my sewing machines are still there and they are the most valuable items. But, I'll check and let you know. 'Bye."

I called Brandy to come back in; I wanted her to go with me just in case somebody was hiding in the studio. She wasn't any sort of an attack dog, but she would stand and bark and hopefully keep any prowler away from me. Her size and her big voice made her seem ferocious, anyway.

Brandy ran into the studio and explored the whole space, nose to the floor. She woofed a couple of times, but then ran back to me, wondering what the rest of this new game was about. It was obvious from her behavior that there was nobody hiding anywhere. Still, it was hard for me to take those few steps out of my secret door's hidey hole into the studio. I made the same tour as Brandy and found nobody. The front door to the outside was closed, but at my touch it swung open. I could see where the doorknob and lock was punched apart. I pushed a table in front of the door to keep it closed. I went back into the house and called Crime Check. The deputy Marty told me he would send out came and looked around and took another report from me. He checked for fingerprints on the door and a couple of the fabric boxes but found only smudges.

"Whoever came in here probably was wearing gloves," he said. "There's not much more I can do. Let us know if you find anything missing or if you think of anything else."

"Okay," I said. "Is it okay to get the door fixed and pick things up, then?"

"You might just as well. It's lucky you weren't here when the perp broke in, anyway. There's nothing for me to use to help catch the guy. It's too bad, but that's often the case."

I watched the deputy drive away then called Gary's Key and Lock to have him come and fix the doorknob and lock. I decided to have a dead bolt put on the door, too. It was a metal door, maybe that would have stopped the intruders if one had been in place the day before.

Then feeling more brave, I started to pick up the mess.

Fabric boxes were emptied out on the floor and the contents pawed through. The gadget drawers in the sewing machine cabinets had been opened, but thankfully not dumped. That would have been a real nightmare. As it was, I spent the rest of the day sorting and repacking fabric boxes. But, there is always a pony, no matter how deep the pile of horse manure you have to dig through. I found fabrics I forgotten I had and felt some project urges coming on. Soon there were stacks of material sitting on the table against the back wall, quilts-to-be.

Gary came to fix the lock and worked while I continued to sort through things and put them away. The light was starting to fade in the windows by the time I hung the last of Barbara's quilts back on the overhead beams. I damp-mopped the floor and then plopped down by the pot-bellied stove. I was beat, but the place was cleaner and neater than it had been since I moved in.

I still had no idea what anybody would be looking for, though. If I had been the intruder I would at least have taken the small sewing machines, those could be sold for a little, if all they wanted was money. But, as far as I could tell there was nothing missing. Marty called back and said he was still busy at the office and wondered if I needed him to come by. I told him no, that while the place was a mess, nothing was gone or damaged, except for the door.

"I called the break-in to Crime Check. They gave me a case number I could use if I had any more information for them and I told them that a deputy you sent had stopped by. Now I'm not sure what to think; what could somebody have been looking for, anyway? Thanks Marty. I'll talk to you later."

I made certain my new door locks were secure, then I went in to take a shower and rustle up some dinner for myself and the animals.

CHAPTER 19

▼

Nothing exciting happened for several days, which was a relief. It was the Wednesday that Rick and his mother were due to arrive and I was just leaving for lunch when the phone rang.

"Hi, Maggie. We're back," Rick said. "I'm going to take the rest of the day off to get her settled. I'll call you or stop by your place as soon as I can."

"I'm so glad you got back okay," I said, "I bet you are exhausted."

"Yes, I am. It was an awful drive. I'll talk to you soon. 'Bye."

Rick showed up at my door on Friday evening, his suitcase in his hand and looking both sheepish and annoyed.

"Would it be alright if I moved in with you for a while?" he asked. "My mother flatly refused to even consider staying in a hotel or motel even after I offered to put her up at The Davenport. She insists on staying with me. As you know, my apartment is tiny, to say the least. I don't think I could do one more night on my love seat. My legs feel like they've been chopped off at the knees."

I took his suitcase away from him and hugged him close, reveling in his delicious aroma.

"You don't even need to ask. Of course, I would like you here forever, you know that."

"I was starting to wonder," he said. "I don't want to push you, but ..."

"Silence, man," I said, then used my lips to still his. "I said yes, that I would marry you, but I just wasn't sure about the when part." And I'm still not, said that shaky little voice in my head, but one step at a time.

"Now, tell me," I said, "What are the plans?"

He shook his head. "Got any coffee? I could really use some of the real stuff. Mom has been feeding me decaf, and weak decaf at that."

"Sure, I'll get some going. That sounds good to me, too."

By the time I had the coffee made and poured, Rick was sitting in one of my recliners with his head leaning back. Both Henry and Cleo were snuggled in his lap and Marmalade perched on one chair arm. Brandy was lying at his feet.

"Here you are, if I can get through all the animals," I said, handing him his coffee.

He sat up and took a long drink, then sighed. "That tastes wonderful. I'll probably be awake all night, but man, it's worth it." His head dropped back as he sighed again.

Yes, I thought, that could be a good thing!

"As to plans, who knows?" he said. "My mother can be so difficult. The best-case scenario would be that she likes my apartment enough to want to stay there. If you meant it about my being here, that would make it easy. Worst case is that she's going to want to spend a bunch of time looking for a place of her own. That'll be hard, poor Jeanne has had to do all the work by herself too much as it is."

Here I go, I thought, Mighty Mouse again: "Here I come to save the day!"

"I could take her around on Tuesdays and Thursdays, if she decides to house hunt," I said.

"Oh, Maggie, I can't ask you to do that."

"You aren't asking, I'm volunteering," I said. "Besides, it could be fun."

Rick snorted. "You haven't met my mother yet. You might change your mind."

"Well, Rose, that's the last one," I said, pushing the sweaty hair off my forehead. Rick was right. This is not as much fun as I imagined. His mother is making me sweat in November.

I looked over at Rose Evans. She sat serenely erect, not a hair out of place, her intricate makeup un-smudged. Her blouse held its shape, somehow. It looked like it had just come off a store's rack, new and unworn. The crease was crisp on her linen slacks, too, how did she keep them from wrinkling? I felt like an unmade bed sitting next to her.

She placed a careful tick mark by the address on the list she held. "You would think a city of this size would have someplace suitable to live," she said, each word roundly stated and dropped into the steamy interior of the Blazer like blobs of butter that started to melt as soon as they landed. All I seem to be able to think about were things melting, me included. "Can't you find me anything better, Maggie?"

Rose had already worn out Brian, the Realtor who found me my Mt. Spokane hideaway, and I was afraid to inflict her on anybody else. I would just keep plugging along until she finally settled on something. But, I didn't think anything would satisfy her antebellum-mansion vision on her simple-little-house-on-a-small-lot budget. I would just have to hope for a miracle.

"I suppose I could just take over Rick's place for good." She gave me a sly look. You don't mind letting him sleep in your spare room, do you?"

I clenched my teeth. She had to know that we are sharing a bed, but chose to feign ignorance. After all, good little Southern girls didn't have sex before marriage, in fact, they didn't really like it much, her curled lip seemed to say. "I'm a damn Yankee!" I wanted to shout at her. "And not only do I like sex in general, I particularly like making love, not just having sex, with your son, so there!" I held my tongue, though. So far I had not done anything to make her mad and I want to keep it that way.

"No, of course I don't mind giving Rick a place to stay. We are going to be married eventually, you know. I may as well get used to having him around."

She considered my answer for a minute, then smiled. Good. I seemed to have dodged another Rose-colored bullet. "Find us a good spot for lunch, Maggie. All this house hunting has made me hungry."

I'm not completely stupid; I knew McDonald's or Burger King would just not do. I took her to the Steamplant Grill, located in the old Spokane steam plant. Much of the steam plant equipment was left in place, cleaned and painted a gleaming black. Metal grill catwalks criss-crossed overhead and every table had a unique view, either of the interior of the old plant itself or of the action going by outside on the sidewalks. The original tall brick chimneys are still there, too. There is a gift shop at the base of one of them and I loved to go into the stack and look up to see the sky that seemed miles above me. Even though many years had passed since the plant was in operation and the chimneys carrying smoke, the aroma lingered. As I hoped, Rose's eyes widened in delight when we walked into the restaurant. She loved the décor, from the mosaic tile in the foyer entry to the machinery inside. I knew the fabulous food they served there would suit her also.

She wiped her mouth and sighed with pleasure. "That was wonderful, Maggie. You found us a perfect spot."

And who said Southern girls don't eat, I thought, looking at the plate she practically licked clean. "I'm glad you liked it," I said. "If you have the energy and as long as we are downtown, there are a couple of condominium buildings nearby that could have some units available that you might like."

Two hours later I dropped Rose off at Rick's apartment. Nothing she had seen quite suited her. She told me again that she might just keep Rick's place, as she had many of her things there already. I didn't care if I never had to look at another prospective home for Rose, but the thought of her choosing Rick's place astounded me. Not that there was anything wrong with his apartment, but it was really just a box in a box, no style or character at all. He told me he considered it just a way station, until he knew for sure if he was going to be staying in the Spokane area.

Lynda Mancusco had helped him make that decision. He was already a prospective partner of Brad's, but after Lynda's death and all the problems with the drug smuggling, Brad moved back to his boyhood home in Oregon. Rick is buying Brad's part of the business and with the client base he had built, he decided to make Spokane his permanent home. It is nice to be a part of that package, I thought. I waved to Rose and drove away toward home.

CHAPTER 20

▼

When I walked in the door Cleo greeted me with her usual glad meows. She spun around the room, weaving between my feet and waving her fluffy tail about. Food! She demanded, FOOD NOW!

Trying not to trip over her, I went to the back room and spooned out some tuna. Brandy was waiting quietly by her dog door, I unlatched it for her and she ran out into the yard.

Marmalade was curled up on the love seat, but where was Henry? I kicked off my shoes and went looking for him.

He was curled up too, on my bed. His head was resting on Barbara's knotty crazy quilt and he was sound asleep. Now how in the world? I knew very well his talent at finding and carrying about objects that he found intriguing, but they usually ran to things like the tube from inside a roll of toilet paper or paper towels, or things he fished out of the waste baskets, wads of paper, bits of fabric, usually nothing that was very large. Plus, I had put this quilt away in the linen closet in the hall.

I went out in the hall and looked and sure enough, one of the linen closet doors was standing open. There were a few towels on the floor too, also no surprise, as I had tucked the quilt away on the back of the shelf behind the towels.

I was sorry I missed Henry getting that quilt out. I know he has a talent for doors; I had long ago stopped being startled by a door that seemed to open by itself. For I knew that when that happened I would see Henry, one black arm stretched out straight in from of him like a ramrod, pushing. So far latched doors eluded him, though. He couldn't quite grip and turn a doorknob. I am rather glad I don't have those latches with handles rather than knobs, or nothing would have been secure.

The catch on this door is a bit loose, though, and that is all that Henry needs. I am sure he jiggled and wiggled things around until finally he could hook his black toes around the door edge and pull it open. Inside the closet the shelves were deep. Henry would have had to have climbed up the shelves to get to the top one, where I had tucked the quilt away. I wondered how he managed to get onto the shelf. It is too high for him to have jumped up. He must have hung like a bat on the lower shelves while he figured out how to get on that top shelf. That must have been quite a sight. I picked up the towels and left him to nap with his prize. If he liked the lumpy thing he could have it.

Rick came home and we soaked in the hot tub before dinner. The deer that were all but invisible all summer long now came every evening to eat the apples that fell off the trees in the back yard. How beautiful those deer were. As I did every fall, I wondered why people felt they had to kill them, or elk, or bears, or whatever. If the need was for food, or self-defense, that I could understand. But, most of the hunters I knew hunted for the thrill of the hunt and the killing, and that was what I could not comprehend—the pleasure in killing. They talked about the camaraderie, the smell of the woods in the fall, the enjoyment of nature. Then why not hunt with a camera? I asked. Why do you have to kill something? They had many answers, but none could answer the what-do-you-enjoy-about-the-killing? question. I gave up asking; it seemed there was no answer.

"So, how did it go with my mom today?" Rick asked.

"About how you warned me it would be. Nothing was just quite right enough for her. She said she may just stay in your place."

"But, why there? It's not a bad place, but it certainly has no style or class," he shook his head. "I don't get it."

"I wondered that myself, but I didn't want to ask her. I was afraid she would agree and then she would want to go on searching. And we have searched. The south side, the north side, the valley, the west plains. I even took her to Cheney, for heaven's sake, thinking the presence of the very impressive Eastern Washington University with its lovely old brick buildings would impress her, but no dice. I'm about at the end of my rope."

Rick chuckled. "Didn't I tell you? But, seriously Maggie, I will be forever grateful to you for taking her on. She is something, isn't she?"

"That hardly describes her. She makes my nit-picky mother look like a saint. I wonder what will happen when those two meet, will it be Greek meets Greek or immediate warfare? I don't think I'm in a hurry to find out."

Rick shuddered. "Me either. You about boiled? Let's go in and get some dinner."

We just finished the last bite when the phone rang. It was Rick's answering service. A horse stepped on a nail, could he please come. With a sigh he struggled into his barn-call overalls. "I hope I won't be too late," he said, kissing me. "Don't wait up for me, though."

CHAPTER 21

▼

"So, Henry, looks like just you and me this evening. I sure wish I could have seen you getting that quilt out of the linen closet." Henry just continued to wash his face. He had nothing to say.

I watched COPS on Court TV, yawning hugely through the last segments. Rick still wasn't back and I couldn't keep my eyes open. Henry kept jumping up in my lap, licking my cheek, then jumping down and heading for the bedroom. He was ready for sleep, too.

I clicked off the TV and stood up. I went over to turn on the lamp by the door and stopped with my hand on the switch. A car was creeping into the driveway, its lights off.

As the car came closer to the house the motion sensors did their job, turning the front of the house into daytime. The car jerked to a stop, then rolled forward a little closer to the house. I could see rust patches fighting for dominance over faded blue paint. I reached into the drawer of the small side table and slid my little Smith and Wesson revolver into my hand. I glanced down to make sure it was loaded and held it down by my leg.

I put the chain on the screen door after Rick left, he would come in through the back door when he got home. If his clothes and boots were muddy he could shed them in the laundry room without walking through the rest of the house. I grabbed the cordless phone with my other hand, tucking it under my arm to free up one of my hands.

A man stepped out of the car and came up onto the porch. A beard hid half his face and he was short and fat. He looked vaguely familiar, but I couldn't place him.

I opened the inside door before he could knock. "Hello, Maggie, long time no see," he said, and smiled.

I slammed the door. The beard covered up most of his face, but those teeth I recognized. It was Norm, Phil's "pal" who had assaulted me. What was he doing out of jail, anyway? Brandy was standing next to me with her side pressed against my leg. The usual mild-mannered dog was growing deep in her throat and the soft short hair on her neck was raised up in a stiff ridge. Henry stood on the back of a chair, every hair sticking out.

Norm banged on the door. "Open up, Maggie, or I kick it in."

I opened the door, the .38 in my hand, safety off and pointed at the center of Norm's chest. "What are you doing here and what do you want?"

"Whoa," he said, stepping back with his hands up. "Don't get excited now, I just have to ask you a question."

"You have about 10 seconds then I'm taking out your kneecaps, you rotten piece of shit," I said. "Talk fast."

I was gratified to hear the tremor in his voice and I hoped he could see the hollow points on the bullets I kept loaded in my pistol. It felt really good to have the upper hand with this man who had for a short time taken away my desire to live.

"Phil just asked me to come get his quilt," Norm said, stepping off the porch and off the side of the driveway, stumbling in the gravel along the edge. "That's all I want."

He probably thinks he is safe, I thought with grim satisfaction. He doesn't know about the hours I spent at Sharp Shooters, the firing range and gun shop at the corner of Trent and Freya, just behind The Crossroads Restaurant, honing my small arms skills.

"What are you talking about; what quilt? I don't have anything of Phil's."

Beads of sweat stood out on Norm's face. "He said it was one a friend made for him, Barbara Hughes? I asked her brother; he said you bought all of Barbara's quilts."

Now my knees felt weak. Had this asshole killed Sam Hughes? And had he searched my quilt studio, too? "Yes, I bought a box of quilts from Sam, but I don't think any of them were made for Phil."

"Phil said it was a small quilt and that she wrote on the back that it was for him."

Norm was talking about the crazy quilt with all the knots on it. I wondered why it was so important to Phil. It wasn't big enough even to use on a prison bed. Besides, I didn't want to do anything to make Phil happy.

"I have looked at all the quilts I bought from Sam, and none of them are addressed to Phil. They all say things on them like for the guest room or the bedroom. Plus, they are all big ones. Now, get out of here and don't come back. I'm calling 911 right now." I held up the phone and started punching buttons with my thumb.

Norm took another step back and tripped in the gravel along the edge of the paved driveway, nearly falling down. "If you have that quilt you'll be sorry you didn't give it to me," he yelled. "And that little peashooter you have don't scare me."

I jerked the chain off the door, poked my hand out the opening, and fired. A burst of shattered rocks danced around Norm's feet and I was gratified to see him leap in the air, frightened at the deliberate near miss. He jumped in his car and spun around in the driveway, gravel flying. I heard his tires chirp as he made the turn onto the road and sped away. Brandy stopped growling, but stayed pressed against my leg.

At some point during the encounter Henry got off the chair and jumped onto the small table. He got down now and went over to where he could look out a window. He curled his lips back and spit so hard his ears laid back. Every hair on his normally sleek body still stuck straight out; he looked like a hedgehog.

I put the safety back on my gun, then blew away the wisp of smoke I imagined I could see drifting out of the barrel. I wished I were wearing a holster, so I could spin the little revolver around on my finger and onto my hip. I cleaned my gun, reloaded the one spent cylinder, and set it down on the table. The barrel was still hot and I would put it away when I was certain it was cool. No sense burning down the house.

"That took care of him. Pretty cool, eh?"

Henry looked at me with dilated black eyes. "Yeow," he said.

CHAPTER 22

▼

I was reaching up to secure the chain back across the door when Rick pulled in. I waited for him to lock up his truck, then held the door open for him.

"Don't touch me, I stink," he said, careful not to brush against me as he walked in. He saw my gun sitting on the table where I had put it. "What the hell ...?"

"Go shower off the barn smells and I'll tell you a story."

"So, I fired one round in the ground, really made him dance." My stomach had almost stopped fluttering, but the big gulp of coffee with a jolt of Kahlua in it I had just sent its way sure helped.

Rick paced back and forth in the living room. "I'm never leaving you here alone at night again," he said, his voice shaking.

"I don't think we need to go that far," I said. "That's why I spent so much time and ammo at the shooting range, so I could safely use my gun to protect myself. Besides, I don't think Norm will be back."

"But he didn't get what he came for." Rick stared at Barbara's lumpy quilt that I had gotten out to show him. "Why does he want that thing, anyway?"

"Supposedly darling Phil sent him to get it. Barbara did sort of make it for him, at least according to what she wrote on the back." I turned the quilt over and showed Rick the faint line of writing that I had shown to Marty. "Besides, if Phil is desperate enough to send Norm out to get it, it must be important in some way. I can't imagine he wants it as a memento of Barbara."

Rick flopped into a chair. "I suppose. But, I still don't like the thought of people coming around here and threatening you."

I suddenly remembered that I totally forgot to tell Rick about the studio being searched. "You know what else? I don't think Norm will be back after I said I didn't have the quilt. Will all the stuff going on with your mom, then you getting called away tonight, and everything else, I forgot to tell you that somebody broke into the studio and searched it."

Rick leaped back to his feet. "You *forgot* to tell me? How could you forget a thing like that?"

"Please don't be mad. It was nothing, really. Someone just went in and poked through things. Nothing was taken, and Marty told me to call in a report to Crime Check. But, all of Barbara's quilts were thrown around, and after Norm's visit tonight, I bet he was the one who did it. He was looking for this." I pointed to the crazy quilt covered with French knots.

"And you didn't think this was important enough to tell me about?" Rick said, red-faced.

"Look, I'm sorry, okay? For years I have just had myself to worry about; I'm still getting used to having you around here all the time. There has just been so much other stuff ..." I realized, appalled, that tears were streaming down my face.

"Oh, Maggie, don't cry." Rick pulled me to my feet and held me close. "But, damn it woman, I love you and I worry about you. Fending off bad guys with a gun, for God's sake."

"That's why I learned how to shoot." I sniffled into his shirt for a minute. "I love you, too, Rick. This is just all so new."

"I know you had a bad time before," he said, his voice tight. "Well, I am a different guy, Maggie. It's time you started to believe that."

I nodded and made a decision. "I know and I do. Tomorrow evening, if you're not too tired, or maybe Saturday, I have something else to tell you about." It was time to show Rick the basement safe house.

"What? Tell me now!" he said, holding me at arm's length so he could look into my face.

"We don't have enough time tonight, and it's nothing scary, okay? Tomorrow or Saturday. We'll need more time and energy that we have right now. Let's go get some sleep."

Rick sighed. "Okay. But, I ..."

"Shhhhh," I said, "Tomorrow evening or Saturday, please?"

CHAPTER 23

▼

Saturday morning if we had chickens Rick would have been up before them. I awoke to the sounds of the espresso machine in the kitchen and knew he would soon be in with a steaming cup for me. He had been totally frustrated to get called out again the night before, he was dying to hear my secret. But, it had turned into a late call; I was asleep when he got home and just barely remembered him sliding under the covers next to me. Funny, the king size bed Phil and I shared hardly seemed big enough. If I touched Phil by accident he would pull away from me, even in his sleep, but this queen size seemed plenty roomy for Rick and me plus a cat or two—and like me, Rick was no midget.

I snuggled down under the covers. This hobo quilt I had made last winter was wonderful; nothing quite like flannel on a chilly morning. I heard the furnace come on; the rest of the house would be warmer than the bedroom where the heat register was closed. I got up and slipped into a bathrobe and went to the kitchen.

"You didn't have to get up," said Rick, handing setting a cup of foamy coffee in front of me and leaning forward with a kiss. "I would have brought this in to you."

"I know," I said, taking a grateful sip, "But it's so warm and cozy out here."

Rick sat down and we watched the birds flutter about the feeders for a few minutes. "So, what's this big secret?"

I bit my tongue to stifle a laugh. He was like a kid on Christmas morning. "Well, it's something I'll show you as soon as we've had some breakfast," I said, "But, in a nutshell, we are sitting on an entire other house, although when you see it you will probably agree with me that it feels more like an apartment."

"What, you mean …?" he pointed down at the floor.

"Yup, the basement."

"But, I've been downstairs and I never saw anything like that."

"No, you wouldn't have, because you weren't supposed to. Anyway, you were only in the utility room."

"I thought that wall all there was to the basement," Rick said, frowning.

"That's what I thought initially, too. Remember what I told you about how I bought this place? How I had to fill out an application and be approved as a buyer? And I told you about Eleanor and Larry Branson, who built it and then when Larry died Eleanor sold it to me and moved away."

Rick nodded. "So?"

"A few days after I moved in Eleanor called me. You know the secret door that goes into the studio out of the kitchen?"

He nodded again, "The one behind the pantry?"

"Yes. Well, there's a whole lot more. There are other ways to get into this safe part down below us from the house, from the living room, from the mud room, to the outside from the utility room, and another one from the studio. Larry really wanted to be able to keep his family safe. There's a security system, too." I pointed to the small black dot in the corner of the kitchen molding up by the ceiling. "That's one of the cameras."

Rick's head turned back and forth. "Cameras? You got this place full of cameras?"

I want to laugh, but I don't. Poor guy. He looked totally spooked. "Just in some strategic places outside, in here, the dining room, living room, and the back porch/mud room parts," I said. "The bedrooms and bathrooms don't have cameras."

"Well, that's a load off my mind. Now, what other secrets are you keeping?"

I looked at his now-angry face in dismay. His reaction didn't really surprise me, but it worried me, too.

"Like you said the other day, I went through some really bad times. The last time I let somebody all the way in to my heart I suffered enormously. But, now I am ready to let you in, but you need to understand and forgive my hesitancy."

This felt like an acid test. How he responded now could mean a wonderful new life, or back to the beginning with just my cats and me. Of course I would need to find another job … I held my breath.

He blew out a big sigh. "There's nothing to forgive, Maggie. I won't lie to you and tell you that it doesn't bother me that you couldn't immediately trust me, but I can understand why you didn't. After all, I am the only one who knew I could be trusted."

I felt my eyes fill and brushed the tears away before he could see them. He passed the test.

I got up and started some bacon frying. "Let's eat and then I'll take you on an adventure," I said.

I started the basement tour by showing Rick the stairs behind the bookcase in the living room. This I thought of as the main way down, as it was the easiest staircase to navigate. The ones from the mud room and out of the studio were steeper and more like ladders. When we got to the bottom his eyes were as wide as mine must have been on my first trip. He looked at the big living/dining room and kitchen area, even opening the small dishwasher and refrigerator like he couldn't believe they weren't toys. He sat on the beds in the two small, functional bedrooms, and turned on the tap in the bathroom, looking astounded when water came out.

"I don't believe this," he said, as he stared out into the utility room through the portal I showed him that opened up into it. "This guy must have been truly nuts."

"No," I said, "He just cared about his family."

"How did you ever figure all this stuff out?" Rick asked, staring at the security monitor in one of the bedrooms.

"Larry made a tape, like one of those self-touring ones you can get when you travel. He led me through the whole place, showed me all the secret doors and passages, and told me how to alert Sonitrol if there is a problem. Remember when those drug smugglers searched the house looking for that lost baggie of cocaine? I was able to get in here and start the cameras rolling. Too bad they only caught a view of the backside of the bad guys, but at least I learned that the system really did work."

"So, those cameras upstairs aren't always on?"

"No, they can only be activated from down here. But, after Norm showed up the other night I'm thinking I want to have a way to start them from upstairs and alert Sonitrol that there's a problem. It would have been nice to have caught Norm on tape or to know who was in the studio that day. Larry hadn't put any cameras in the shop area, either, but now I think we need them there, too."

"That is a great idea. I was going to suggest a security system after you told me about the studio break-in anyway, but maybe this one can just be upgraded."

"I'm sure it can. Now, Rick, you are the only other person besides Eleanor Branson and me to know about this, except for Sonitrol, of course. I think we need to keep it that way. Marty doesn't even know about it."

"But, you told him you had seen …"

"Yes," I interrupted him. "But what I told Marty and the other cops is that I was able to peek in a back window and just saw the guys leaving out the front. That's what I told Sully too, after she took a shot at them."

At times I swore I could still taste the dirt I ate when I hit the ground that evening. Sully, my neighbor from up the road, saw a strange car in my driveway and came to investigate, shotgun in hand. She let fly with a load of buckshot when she realized the men had broken into my house. The noise of the blast sent me diving for cover, my face in the gravel. It was too bad she missed the car, but it was nice to know somebody was watching out for me, too.

I led Rick to the steep set of stairs that opened up into the mud room. Then I showed him the passage from in the studio. He already knew about the hidden back door in the studio that opened to the outside. We went back to kitchen for another cup of coffee.

"Whew," he said. "That was amazing. And not a single sign of that place from the outside. Even with no windows it didn't feel claustrophobic at all."

"I know. Isn't it something? I'll call Sonitrol on Monday and talk to them about doing something upstairs. Maybe a code pad by the doors and panic buttons in every room? How does that sound? I don't think motion detectors on the inside would be a very good idea, Brandy and the cats would have the cops here all the time and all the wildlife around would set them off in the back all the time, too. I think the motion lights and the cameras we can activate outside are enough for now."

Rick nodded. "Yeah, you're probably right about that. We could do the same type of system we have at the office. Let's just reverse the order of the office code numbers, then it won't be so hard to remember the code for home."

"That makes sense. I'll see what Sonitrol can do for us."

CHAPTER 24

▼

Too soon it was Monday and time to go back to work. Jeanne had a fairly calm on-call weekend, just a mom cat with a little trouble with her first litter of kittens and a puppy that ate a non-toxic houseplant, panicking its owners. Rose had not called on Rick all weekend either. All that made the new week easier to face.

I called and talked to Sonitrol. They said they would send someone out the next day to discuss upgrading my current security system.

Rick and Jeanne had an appointment with the clinic's tax accountant at the end of the day, so I snuck away a little early. After a couple of trials riding to work together, Rick and I realized that was not always going to work out. It seemed if there was only one car between us Rick would have to go on a farm or house call, leaving me to beg a ride from Jeanne or wait for him at the clinic. He also carried lots of supplies in his truck and sometimes I had trouble finding a place to sit. Now we both drove our own vehicles to work. Today I was glad about this again; I could go straight home.

The mailbox held a treat, a letter from my sister, Beth. The envelope was covered with Irish postage stamps and had a nice heft to it. Probably some more pictures of the kids, I hoped.

Beth and I tried to stay in touch, emailing frequently and having occasional phone conversations. But, the time difference between here and Ireland is always a problem, so those calls are rare. I put her letter down; I would open it and read it as soon as I had dinner started.

I put a chicken on to cook and went looking for the cats. Most days they greeted me at the door, but I was early today and caught them napping.

Cleo and Marmalade were in the bay window in the dining room, watching the birds. Henry was on my bed, he had again dragged Barbara's odd little quilt up there from where I had put it on a chair. He was standing on the quilt, rubbing his face against the French knots.

"Those are good to rub an itch against, aren't they?"

He looked up briefly, said "Mummmmmmpf," and went back to rubbing his face, first one side and then the other. I watched him for a minute then picked him up.

"Do we have a flea problem here again?" I said, sitting down with him in my lap and sorting through the fur on his face and neck. I had gone through a spate of flea infestations not long after I moved in. Henry had what Brad had told me was an allergic-like reaction to flea bites. He broke out in crusty areas anywhere that he was bitten. Once I got rid of the fleas, Henry's skin healed and has been fine ever since.

His skin was still intact. No sign of a flea bite anywhere and when I parted the short fur on his tummy I saw no little brown bugs moving about or any of their miniscule droppings. I stroked smooth the streak of white fur on his left shoulder where a bullet had grazed him while we were staying at my aunt Lola's place. Henry seemed to have the same talent for trouble that I did. The bullet took out a strip of skin, and the fur grew back white instead of the black coat he wore on the rest of him. It gave him a bit of a rakish air that I liked.

"No fleas, big guy." I let him go and he went back to rubbing his face on the knots. "Oh, well, whatever makes you happy."

I left him to his pleasures and went to get the rest of dinner on the stove.

With chicken Cacciatora bubbling happily away I sat down with Beth's letter. Sure enough, she had sent photos of my niece and nephew, now two and five years old. She also sent pictures of her latest landscaping efforts around her old stone cottage. In one picture she stood grinning widely next to a trellis loaded with climbing roses. She had really taken to gardening after moving to Ireland.

I thought back to how all that happened. Beth had gone on a People-to-People tour in the summer before her senior year of high school. The tour took them through several European countries and in Ireland she met Patrick Shaunessy, Paddy to all his friends. He was manning a booth of fruit and vegetables at a farmer's market and they started talking about apples. Being from Washington State, one of the apple capitals of the U.S., Beth was a great source of information for him. They exchanged addresses and both of them promised to write.

Beth came home with stars in her eyes and dreams of love in her young heart. My mother, in her typical wonderful way, did all in her power to destroy Beth's hopes. "All he wants is one thing … you didn't …" My mother stopped talking, horrified at the thought.

"We hardly had the opportunity, mother," Beth had answered, "Not that I would tell you, anyway."

Good for you, I silently cheered. It's about time you stood up to her.

"Well, you best not pin any hopes on this boy," my mother went on. "He will never write back to you anyway."

My mother was proven wrong. Beth went on to college, but she and Paddy kept in contact. He finally was able to make a trip to the United States and he and Beth spent a lot of time together. I was glad that Beth was away from home or I am sure my mother would somehow have tarnished the growing love she and Paddy were finding with each other.

I don't what my mother could have found to dislike about Paddy, but she would have dug up something. When I first met him I was delighted with the way he treated Beth, what a gentleman he was. Those brilliant blue eyes sparkling from under a generous head of black curly hair didn't hurt either. By the time he and Beth came to Spokane and he met my mother, the decisions were already made. Beth knew that the only way she could have the sort of wedding she wanted would be to plan the whole thing out and have it paid for by the time our mother knew anything about it.

How right she had been, too. I was already living in Seattle when Beth and Paddy announced their plans. Beth told me later how Mother had smiled and approved of everything, at least to Beth's face, when she and Paddy described all the arrangements they made. But, there were many ugly scenes later, Beth said, that I was glad I missed. The long distance phone lines did almost melt, though, from the number of calls that came my way.

Then after the wedding when Beth and Paddy announced they would be living in Ireland Mother really went nuts. But, the plane tickets were bought and Beth had already sent ahead all of her clothes and various household items she bought for her hope chest. In the end all Mother could do was kiss her good-bye. I fled back to Seattle as soon as I could.

Beth and I both felt guilty about distancing ourselves from our mother, especially after our dad died. But, she pretty much brought it upon herself. It was too hard constantly trying to please her and just as constantly failing. I was glad she seemed to have found a new home in San Diego.

Beth's letter went on with more news of her life. She saved the bombshell until the last paragraph.

"Mom wrote and told me she is planning on moving back to Spokane. Has she said anything to you?"

CHAPTER 25

▼

All three cats were at attention, the fur standing up along their spines. Brandy got up too, and was watching me intently. I realized that I had leaped to my feet and yelled, "She's WHAT?" Beth's letter flying out of my hands.

"Sorry, guys," I said, gathering up scattered paper. "It's okay; I was just surprised by something." Brandy walked over to me, stiff-legged. I patted her until she relaxed and went back over to curl up on her quilted dog pad in the corner. Henry settled right back down, but it took Cleo and Marmalade several minutes before they allowed their fur to smooth out. All three of them then started to bathe their coats; like they were trying to wash away their fear.

Fear. Perfect word. The thought of my mother being back in Spokane, where she could come and see me, and easily call me day or night, scared the crap out me. I hoped this was just an off-hand comment to Beth, but in my hearts of hearts I knew better. My mother did not make those kind of comments very often.

I picked up Beth's letter and sat back down. Henry crawled up into my lap; he knew I was upset about something.

"Oh, Henry, what are we going to do?" I absently stroked his sleek back and he licked my arm. "She will drive me crazy; I just know it."

I sat and stared across the room for several minutes. I was just going to have to be very busy and keep our contacts to a minimum. I would have to remember not to tell her anything I wanted, planned, needed, or was concerned about, because she would interfere. My wants would be unnecessary, my plans not good, my needs not important and my worries? Either she would discount them as trivial, or obsess on them, calling me with endless "solutions" that I was to implement immediately. I sighed. At least I knew what could happen and hopefully she wouldn't be able to get to me like she had when I was a child. She always found the chink in my armor, that was the trouble.

I got up to check on the Cacciatora. It smelled wonderful and made the whole house into an Italian restaurant. The chicken and tomato sauce would go on a bed of spaghetti. I would steam some broccoli and make a couple of pieces of garlic toast to go with the pasta. Sometimes I went all out and made my own spaghetti sauce, but tonight I had taken the easy way. I just pulled the skins off four chicken thighs and cooked them just a bit on each side in a dab of olive oil. Then I poured a jar of commercial sauce over the thighs, covered the pan and put them in a 350-degree oven for about an hour. So easy and so good.

I had just pulled the bread out from under the broiler when I heard Rick come in the back door. I let him eat before I told him about the possibility of my mother moving back to Spokane.

"You don't sound too happy," he said.

"I've told you what she's like. You think *your* mother is bad; wait until you meet mine."

"I've met her, remember?"

"Yeah, but that didn't count. When you guys met you were just the employee of my boss, at least that's how she saw you. Besides, at that time she was still trying to get me to get back with Phil, so she didn't bother to take too many shots at you. Now that you're living here and we have plans, though, watch out!"

Rick got up off the couch where he had been lounging with Cleo in his lap. He took hold of my hands to get me to stop pacing around the room and pulled me down to sit next to him.

"It'll be okay," he said.

"How do you figure?"

"Well," he stopped and looked away from me. "I wasn't going to tell you this right now, because it's still a few weeks away, but I may not be here when she gets here, if she comes."

"What? Where are you going to be?" Now I was feeling abandoned as well as fearing having to defend myself every minute.

"Several of us on the veterinary council have decided to go and spend a month or so in the gulf coast area. There are so many animals that were victims of the hurricanes that some of us decided to go and do what we could for them. You know Bob Olson? His brother is a vet down there and Bob was telling us how overwhelmed they all are. So …"

I gulped, trying to swallow the lump in my throat so I could talk. "When were you going to tell me about this, the day before you left?"

"No, of course not. We just made this decision a couple of days ago at our lunch meeting. I hadn't said anything because we still aren't sure exactly when we will be leaving, but it won't be for a month or so, or maybe even longer. The plans are not really firmed up yet."

"Great. My mother may show up, your mother is already here and you're leaving Jeanne and me in the lurch again." I didn't want to sound cranky, but I was cranky, and hurt.

Rick shook his head. "No, it's not like that. I talked to Jeanne first, before I told the guys I would come with them," he said. "She wanted to go, too, but with her little one at home she doesn't feel like she could leave right now. She is happy that I'm going to go and help them out."

"You talked to Jeanne, you talked to everybody but me?" I heard my voice sail up to a tiny squeak. I took a deep breath and held it. I blew it out and sighed. "I'm sorry to sound mad, Rick. But, it seems like so much is going on, what with Phil and his quilt, your mother, my mother, I'm worried about Georgia, just so much."

"You'll do okay, Mags, you always hold it all together."

"Yeah, I suppose I will. It all just seems like too much and at times I just get really tired keeping all the balls in the air."

Rick got up. "I have faith in you," he said. "I'm going to go check my email. Bob is checking on plane tickets for us and said he would let us know as soon as he has some information."

I watched Rick walk into my office. I like being strong, I like being able to cope, the clinging vine type has never been my personality. But, every now and then I want to be able to give it all up, let somebody else take the reins and take care of me for a change. I felt tears blur my eyes and blinked furiously to take them away. I didn't want to be seen as a sniveler, especially when Rick was doing something that was so noble.

Henry jumped up on the couch next to me and dropped a catnip mouse in my lap.

"Meow," he said, and to me it sounded like, "I'll take care of you."

CHAPTER 26

───────────── ▼ ─────────────

As Sonitrol promised, their estimator was on time Tuesday morning. It only took him a few minutes of looking at my present system to determine that it would be easy to wire the main floor rooms with panic buttons. After talking to him about the door alarms, I decided to put alarms on the windows too. If they were opened without a release button being pushed, like if they were forced open from the outside, that would set off an alarm, too. I hadn't even thought about the windows before, but if I were going to be here by myself again it made good sense.

The Sonitrol man flipped open his appointment book. "We can do everything on Thursday, if you can give us the whole day."

"That would be great," I told him, "What time do you want to start?"

Thursday morning Rick and I got up early. We took the cats downstairs and closed them in the bedroom that did not have the security monitor in it. Sonitrol said they only needed to get into the one room with the monitor, so the cats would be safe. I wasn't really worried about Henry, but he would have driven the installer crazy, trying to "help" him, either by riding on the man's shoulders or sticking his black nose into everything. He wouldn't be happy being away from the action, but too bad. Cleo and Marmalade would probably spend their day under the bed, eyes black with anxiety.

Brandy would be fine in the back yard. Rick went to work and I puttered about, waiting for Sonitrol to show up.

The installer started in the studio, putting a video camera into each corner. The cameras wouldn't be able to see the whole place due the exposed beams and the quilts hanging over them, but they would still show if anybody came in the doors or the windows. After the installation was done, I tried to work on a baby quilt I was commissioned to make, but found myself unable to stay focused. I wandered back to the house and I was glad to see Sully, my neighbor from up the road, headed to the front door.

"Whatcha doin' here?" she asked.

"Just having the security system upgraded."

"I figured you was up to something, what with the truck in the driveway. Want to come up for lunch?"

Normally a session with Sully was exhausting. She was like a brain Hoover, sucking every thought right out of my head. But, even that seemed preferable to fidgeting around at home while Sonitrol worked. I told the man where he could reach me and walked up to Sully's house with her.

The landscaping hadn't improved since I first saw it. Sully kept her grass mowed, but didn't bother with much else. The surrounding forest pushed in on all sides, tree branches brushing against the steep roof of her old A-frame house. Buffy greeted me with his usual vigor. I assumed the end that was wiggling the most frantically must be the tail end, so aimed my pats at the opposite end. How this dog could see, eat, or do anything through the blanket of hair all over him, I never understood.

"Looks like Rick has moved in, huh?" Sully said, with a lascivious leer.

"Yes. His mother came to town and she is living in his apartment until she can find a place of her own. But, that has been a futile task so far. I have spent several days taking her around to look at places, but she can't seem to find anything that is just right." I sighed. "She's a bit of a Southern belle, at least in her estimation. The trouble is, she wants Tara on a *The Waltons* budget."

Sully handed me a roughly made sandwich and a bowl of thick soup. She made her own breads and soups, and while they might look odd, I knew they would be delicious. The first bite of each confirmed this.

"Thanks for lunch, Sully. This is great."

She grinned. She loved the compliment, but she would ignore it. "Oh, it's just some things I threw together."

I knew she meant this, too. I asked for a soup recipe once and she couldn't give me one. Just gave me some vague directions about putting this and that together. I knew better than to even attempt it.

"So, you got Rick moved in. When's the big day?"

The Hoover was on. "I don't know yet. We are trying to get Rose settled, that's his mother's name, by the way, and then we can make some plans. Every time he says anything around her about us getting married, though, she changes the subject. I can't imagine her approving of her son 'living in sin,' but she doesn't seem to want us married, either."

"Is Rick a mama's boy? Is he going to let her run his life?" Sully was indignant.

"No, I don't think so," I said. "He is trying to be extra kind to her right now, though, because she did just lose her husband."

"Hmmpf," said Sully. "I seen them at the store the other day and I wondered who the woman was. She was ordering him around pretty good."

"Well, you know how it is with moms and kids; no matter how old the kid." I needed to change the subject. "Looks like you've made some changes around here," I said, looking around. Sully's living room used to be a testament to her late husband's love for hunting. I think he was spouse number four, but I'd lost track. There had been deer, elk, and moose heads, stuffed and hanging all around the room. There had been various antlers mounted on plaques and displayed as well, but all the trophies were gone. The bear rug from in front of fireplace was gone, too. When I first met Sully she told me several stories about various good times she and her last husband enjoyed on that rug, images I really did not want. Now the floor gleamed from a recent sanding and varnishing. She had put several area rugs around, in warm tones with accents of forest green and maroon. Now all she needed was a quilted wall hanging. That would be her Christmas present, I decided. She mentioned wanting one once, so I knew it would be a good gift. Maybe I would make a pillow to go with it. Then a lap quilt would do for her birthday. I had some fabric with deer on it that would be perfect for her.

"Yeah, what do you think? It looks a little different, don't it. I liked them heads up there, but when I took them down to paint I liked the way it looked so much that I sold them all, and all the antlers too. I put the bear rug on the back porch for Buffy; he really likes it."

"It looks great, Sully, a real improvement. So much lighter and brighter. What's going on around the mountain these days, anyway?"

For the next two hours Sully regaled me with stories of the people who lived near us, and even some not so near, in the Mt. Spokane foothills. I didn't even try to remember the tales; I didn't have the steel-trap mind that Sully did. That was probably a good thing, though. There were several stories I wouldn't want to recall if I ran into the people who starred in them.

I got back home just in time for the Sonitrol man to show me how the upgraded system worked. It looked like it was going to be easy to use and would give me more protection here in my somewhat isolated house. I to waved good-bye to the Sonitrol installer and hurried downstairs to let the cats out of their prison.

CHAPTER 27

▼

I started a roast cooking, then went into the bedroom and plopped down on the bed, Henry next to me on his quilt. At least somebody liked Barbara's lumpy project. I laid there and looked out the skylight, watching the sky darken toward evening. Rick would be home soon and I could show him the new system. It occurred to me that Marty might want to know about Norm's visit. I rolled over and grabbed the phone.

"I forgot to tell you, Marty," I told his voice mail, "Remember that Norm guy I told you about? Phil's pal? Well, he is obviously out of jail as he paid me a visit. It seems that Phil wants that quilt that I showed you. I wonder if Norm was the guy who broke into my studio …"

"Maggie?" Marty's voice broke in. "I just got back to the office. I left the phone on speaker and I could hear you. What's this about that Norm guy?"

"He showed up at my door a few nights ago. He said he had come for Phil's quilt; that ugly little thing I showed you."

"Did you give it to him?"

"No, I told him I didn't have anything that belonged to Phil. He didn't ask about any of the others, that's what made me think he had already looked at them."

"I wonder what is so special about that quilt," Marty said.

"Yeah, me too. When Norm started to get abusive I scared him away with my .38."

"Oh, Lord, Maggie, be careful. He could have taken it away from you and shot you."

"I just stuck my hand out through the door and fired a round into the dirt by the driveway. Really made him dance. I wonder, though, could he have been the guy who killed Sam?"

"I don't know," said Marty, "But we will be taking a close look at him. Do you know his last name?"

"You know, I never did know it. But I am sure that the Seattle police will have it. They might even have DNA from him."

"Thanks, Maggie. We'll look into it. But, you be careful, now. This Norm character doesn't sound like he takes no as an answer very well."

"Okay, Marty, I will. Sonitrol was just here to update the security system and Rick has moved in, too, so that helps."

Henry went out of the bedroom while I talked to Marty. I could hear him chattering around in the kitchen. He was hungry. It was time to add some potatoes and carrots to the roast I had in the oven for Rick and me, too.

"You be sure and keep me posted on anything else that happens, Maggie," Marty said.

"Thanks, Marty, I will." I hung up the phone and got up to go to the kitchen to tend to Henry and the roast.

CHAPTER 28

▼

Tap, tap, tap. With a barely suppressed groan I put down my marking pen. I went and peeked out the small window in the front of the studio and sure enough, Rose's red Ford Taurus was sitting in my driveway.

Not again. This was the third day in a row when I was home that she showed up at my door. I knew she was lonely, but I had work to do. The quilts I had taken in to do for people were starting to stack up. I just did not have the time to sit and listen to Rose tell stories for hours. But, she knew I was home and I couldn't very well ignore her.

"Hi, Rose," I said, opening the door. "How are you today?"

"Hello, Maggie. I'm fine."

As usual, Rose was dressed to hatbox perfection. She had on dark pink slacks and a jacket, with a lighter pink shirt peeking out at the neck. Her gleaming white walking shoes matched the white piping on the jacket. I would not have been surprised to see white gloves and a perky little hat, but I suppose those just 'would not go' with pants.

"So, this is where you make all your wonderful quilts?" she said as she walked in and sat down by the potbellied stove.

"Is this the first time you've been in the studio? I thought I brought you in here when I first showed you the house."

"Oh, we just peeked in the door that day, Maggie. This is the first time I've really been inside."

"I have coffee on in the house," I said. "Let me get you some."

Teeth clenched, I went into the kitchen. "I have to find her a hobby, other than me that is," I muttered as I fixed coffee with cream and sugar. "I can't do this every day I have off from the clinic."

I handed Rose her coffee. "If it's okay with you I'd like to talk while I finish marking this quilt," I said. "My customer wants it back by this weekend so that she can get the binding put on it; it's a wedding gift that she needs ready in a couple of weeks. You'll be comfy by the stove."

"You go ahead, dear. I'll just turn up the heat a bit and toast my toes."

I picked up my water soluble pen and went back to work. The customer wanted the outer border crosshatched. That meant I would sew a straight line at a 45 degree angle from the outer edge of the quilt up to outer edge of the border fabric. The next line of stitches would be one inch from the first line and parallel to it. Once the whole border had these stitch lines on it I would start over, sewing 45 degree lines in the opposite direction. This would cover the border with 1x1 inch quilted squares. Drawing the lines on is only way I could be sure and keep them straight as I moved the machine over the quilt. I had a special thick plastic ruler that I placed over the marks I drew on the quilt top to achieve those straight lines. I could run the presser foot along that ruler like a pencil along a ruler on a piece of paper. The thickness of the plastic kept the hopping presser foot from going over the top of the ruler, which would sew it into the quilt if that happened!

Rose chattered while I marked, telling me more stories about Rick and his childhood. Most of them I had heard by now and all she needed was an occasional uh-huh or "Oh, really?" to keep her happy.

Time flew by and before I knew it the morning was gone. I had a lunch date with Georgia and I was relieved when just moments before I was going to have to convince Rose to leave she stood up.

"Well, this has been nice," she said. "But, I better get home and do my laundry. Thanks for the coffee, Maggie."

"You're welcome," I said. The minute her car pulled out of my driveway I dashed into the house. Within seconds I changed out of my sweats and tossed on a pair of slacks and a shirt. I would be early meeting Georgia for lunch, but I wouldn't mind waiting. I wanted to be gone in case Rose decided to come back. She had done that the last time she stopped in. She ended up staying for lunch and dinner and I wondered if she were going to spend the night, too. I needed to find SOMETHING for her to do and the sooner the better.

"What about the Senior Citizens' Center there in that new Mirabeau complex?" Georgia suggested after I told her about Rose and her visits.

"I thought of that place and I am going to get her a trial membership at Stroh's, too. Otherwise, I'm going to have to kill her."

Georgia laughed. "Boy, do I ever know what you mean. Ron and I came within an inch of having his mom living with us for the rest of her life."

I remembered the granny flat that Georgia and her husband, Ron, built in their basement. Ron's mother, Nila, was set to move in as soon as she sold her house in Tacoma. Luck was on Georgia's side, though. Nila sold her house in November and by the time she got to Spokane, there were six inches of snow in the ground. That was the start of a long, snowy time. The last of the snow did not melt until after the first of April that year. That was a bit unusual for this area, but Georgia told me it was like the weather knew she needed the help. Nila was tired of the rain-only winters of the west side of the state, but that first winter here in Spokane was a shock and she didn't like it a bit. She called a Realtor in Palm Springs and told him to find her a condo. By summertime she had moved away, much to Georgia's relief.

That granny flat had been a life saver for me, though. After fleeing Seattle, it was wonderful to have a place where I could stay until I could get my bearings. Even the cats were happy. Ron and Georgia put in a dog door leading to a kennel, allowing Henry and Cleo access to the outside. That gave me the idea to put cat door into the dog kennel that came with the house I bought in the Mt. Spokane foothills.

"So, is Marmalade still fat and sassy?" Georgia asked.

"Yes, she is. It took a lot to get her well at first, but since then she has done fine." I remembered what a pathetic little handful of fur-covered bones Marmalade had been when Georgia brought her to the clinic. Her belly swollen with worms, ears black with mites, and nose and eyes running from an upper respiratory infection. It had taken vet help and lots of nursing care to pull her through.

"I'm so glad you were able to take her in," Georgia said.

"Me too. I worried a bit about Cleo, she can be so protective of the kittens she doesn't have and never will have, but I suppose that Marmalade being a female made the difference. They have pretty much been good friends since the beginning."

"That's good. She is such a pretty thing. Well, I'd best get going," Georgia said, with a glance at her watch. "Ron has been out of town for a couple of days and I better see if I can stir up something for dinner that will please him."

"Is anything wrong, Georgia?" I asked. "You seem kind of down."

"Oh, I don't know. Things have been a little off recently, but every time I ask Ron if there is anything wrong all I get is, 'No, everything's fine.' I'm not sure I believe that, though. I just have this feeling ..." Georgia's voice faded and she blinked away sudden tears.

"Let me know if I can help you in any way," I said.

"Thanks, Maggie, I will." Georgia gave me a quick hug then hurried out to her car.

I sat for a minute. I hated to see Georgia unhappy. She and Ron seemed so well suited to each and other and were, at least to my eyes, happy for the years they had been together so far. I hoped so much that things would work out for them. Time will tell, I suppose.

CHAPTER 29

▼

By the time I got home it was time to start dinner for Rick and me. There was roast left over. I would just whip up a salad and some veggies, that would be good, and easy, too.

I tore up lettuce and sliced tomatoes. Henry kept winding around my legs, pearling and talking. I picked him up and set him on the counter where his food bowls are, but that did not seem to please him. Every time I tried to turn to the refrigerator or the stove he was right there, underfoot.

"What IS it?" I asked him; like he could answer me. He stared at me, yellow eyes wide, and pearled again. There was something he needed, but I did not know what it was.

"Do you want to go out, is that it? Did I forget to unlock your cat door?"

I checked the lock on the door that led to the kennel, but it was not locked. I would just have to watch out I didn't step on him, I supposed.

I finished the salads and started the vegetables steaming in the microwave. I turned to go into the other room, but before I could take a step Henry floated up onto the counter and start to rub his face on the phone.

"You need to make a call?" I asked him, laughing. I picked up the receiver and held it out to him.

He bobbed his head, seeming to agree. I leaned down to let him nuzzle my ear and it was then that I heard the beep-beep-beep that signaled a message.

"Were you trying to tell me somebody called?" I asked Henry. But, he jumped to the floor and walked away. His mission was accomplished, his waving tail said.

I punched in the retrieval number and listened—I had one new message.

"Maggie?" said a quavering voice I did not immediately recognize. "This is Sully. Please call this number," she said, then read off some digits. "Please call right away." The connection broke off.

What the hell? This was not a number I recognized and Sully did not sound like herself. With fingers that began to shake, I replayed the message so I could write down the numbers Sully listed and then punched them in.

I let the number ring for five minutes by the clock, but nobody answered. I grabbed my jacket and headed for the door.

Within minutes I was standing on Sully's front porch. I could see Buffy sleeping on the living room couch, but he did not stir when I rang the doorbell, then knocked. But Sully had to be home; her little pickup was in the car port.

I walked around to the back door where I could peek into the kitchen. I could see a broken coffee cup on the floor, but no Sully. What was going on? I turned around and hurried back to my house.

CHAPTER 30

▼

As I unlocked my front door I could hear the phone ringing. I dashed to the kitchen and picked it up.

"You have Phil's quilt ready for me by ten in the morning," a muffled voice said, "Or you can kiss your friend Sully good-bye. Call the cops, and she's dead."

"What, who is this?" I yelled, but only the buzz of a disconnect answered me. I hit *69, but that weird disembodied voice that Qwest uses just said, "The number called cannot be reached." The caller had blocked it.

Sully's been kidnapped? That's what it sounded like. All right, that was enough for me. Phil could have his ugly quilt.

I dashed into the bedroom, expecting to see that garish splash of color on the bed, where Henry had drug it every day. The quilt was not there. I looked around wildly. Henry must have it on the floor, or something. But, there was no sign of the little quilt. Henry, however, was now sitting serenely in my bedroom chair, calmly grooming his whiskers.

"Where's your quilt, Henry? What did you do with it?" He squinted at me then went back to his grooming.

I started to rush around the house, looking everywhere I could think of. Within minutes I had searched everywhere; that quilt was not to be found. I even looked in the back of the linen closet, maybe those clever black paws had put the quilt away.

Now I was getting frantic. I knew if I wasn't looking for it I would be tripping over it. It was too big to hide just anywhere; it had to be here somewhere. I started looking stupid places; in the microwave, under the lid over the toilet tank. I was frantic.

"What are you doing?"

I jumped and hit my head on the underside of the table behind the love seat. I was crawling around the living room with a flashlight in hand, searching for the quilt that Henry loved and had probably hidden.

"Oh, my God, Rick, you scared me. I didn't even hear you come in. Somebody, probably that creep Norm, has kidnapped Sully. He wants that ugly quilt in trade for her, but I can't find it. I've looked everywhere. I need you to help me."

I dropped onto the love seat and rubbed my head, tears threatening.

"Did you call the police?"

"No, not yet. The guy said not to, that I just need to have the quilt ready for him by ten in the morning. I'm about to go nuts here—you have to help me!"

He came over and put his hands on my shoulders. "Calm down, Mag," he said. "First of all, we need to call the police." He walked over and picked up the phone.

With a gymnastic ability that I didn't know I possessed, I vaulted up out of the love seat and launched myself across the room at him.

"No," said, knocking the phone out of his hand. "He said no cops, or Sully would die."

"You know how these things usually turn out, Maggie. Sully may already be dead. We have to call the police."

"Please, just help me find that quilt," I begged. "I have to take the chance that this guy will release Sully if I give it to him. But, I need to find it first." By now I was sobbing and looking again everywhere I had already searched. I started to look in even more stupid places, too, where a quilt would be obvious and where I knew Henry could never have put it. I looked on the book case, on top of the TV, flew out into the kitchen and looked in the oven, the pantry, everywhere, but no luck. Henry "helped," pushing his black furry nose in front of my face over and over. After another fruitless pass through the kitchen I went back out in the living room.

I saw Rick pick up the phone again. "If you make that call, we are through," I said, teeth clenched. "This does not involve you; the call came to me. Just butt out."

Rick set the phone down, his face ashen. "You are involved, Maggie, and that involves me. You could get hurt, dealing with this guy. Please let me help."

"I already told you what I need," I said. "I need to find that quilt."

Rick started to silently search the house. I knew I had hurt him, but I couldn't stop myself. I had to rescue Sully.

CHAPTER 31

▼

By midnight we gave up. It was like that ugly little quilt had just vaporized. I could not imagine where Henry might have hidden it, but it was gone. Exhausted, I finally fell into bed.

The next morning it was all I could do to get up and get ready for work. Ten o'clock would come and I was empty-handed. Sully would die and it would be my fault.

At work it was all I could do to even cope with the tiniest tasks. Even answering the phone seemed too big a job and I had to concentrate on each call. The hands on the clock seemed to stand still for an eternity, then suddenly twitch forward and an hour would be gone.

Just before ten o'clock I saw Sully's little truck pull into the parking lot. She got out and walked across the asphalt like she was walking on eggs. She came in front door and gave me a sickly smile.

"Hi, Maggie. Give me the quilt."

"Sully, I don't have it. I can't find the stupid thing."

Her eyes goggled. "What? But he told me you would have it," she said.

"I know. I thought I would. Henry must have drug it off somewhere. Rick and I tore the house apart last night, but we can't find it anywhere."

I peered out the window and looked at Sully's truck. There did not seem to be anybody in it. Sully must be here by herself. I couldn't see any other cars around, but even if the place was being watched I could take her in the back, hide her in the crematory area somewhere and she would be safe. I came out from behind the counter and took her hand.

"Come with me," I whispered.

"Oh, Maggie, let go. We could both die." Sully pulled her hand out of mine and lifted her shirt. I saw the pipe bomb taped to her abdomen. It looked like there was a beeper attached to it.

"He said if anything goes wrong he will call the beeper number and the bomb will go off. If I try to take it off it will go off, too."

"What are we going to do, Sully?"

"Try to call him," she said. "Here's the number I am supposed to call as soon as I have the quilt. Tell him you can't find it and maybe he will give us more time."

My hands were shaking so hard it took several tries before I was able to punch in the correct numbers. This time the phone only rang once.

"Sully? You got it?"

"No, this is Maggie. Sully is here, but I don't have the quilt. I can't find it; I think my cat drug it off and hid it somewhere in my house. I need more time to look for it."

"Are you screwing around with me? I told you ten o'clock this morning. Do you know all I have to do is send a few numbers out and you and your friend will be toast?"

"Yes, she showed me the bomb. But, I tried to find the quilt, I really did. Please give me more time." I hoped my voice didn't sound as shaky to him as it did to me.

There was a long silence. I was afraid he had just walked away from the phone, but finally his voice came back.

"Okay, but this is your last chance. Tell Sully to go home. I will be waiting there for her. Then tomorrow, by this time, you be at her house with that quilt or you both die. Got that?"

While he talked I could hear footsteps, like he was walking as he talked. I could also hear a noise in the background that was faint, but it became louder then faded again. The sound tickled at my memory; it was something I knew, like something out of my childhood. Just about the time the sound started to get loud enough that I thought I knew what it was it faded away again. Then I heard the sound of a door opening and a latch click, like a door was closing, then there was silence.

"Send Sully home," he said, "Then I will see you both, with that quilt, tomorrow."

CHAPTER 32

▼

I went home early and searched the whole house again. This was ridiculous; where had Henry put that awful quilt? Once again I had to give up. It was not to be found.

I sat down in the middle of the living room floor. I let my head drop down and I wept again, in frustration and heartbreak. Sully would die, I probably would too, and all for nothing. I let the tears flow. Finally, exhausted, I stretched out on the rug, Henry pressed against my side.

I must have fallen asleep, as the sudden ring of the phone had me gasping. How long had it been ringing, anyway? I pushed myself to my feet and staggered across to the phone table. I grabbed the receiver.

"Hello?" I croaked, looking down at the caller ID box. It said the call was blocked, but before I could hang up I heard somebody talking.

"Maggie, it's Sully," came a quivering voice. "He let me call you so I could tell you about feeding Buffy."

"Are you all right?"

"I am for now. Buffy will be hungry and I need you to go feed him, but I am out of dog food."

"Sully, is he listening in?"

"No, not really."

"Are you home?"

"No. I will need you to feed Buffy."

"Is he right there, can he hear you, Sully?"

"Yes, like I said, I am out of dog food. You will have to go to Tidyman's, the one here in the VALLEY, on McKinnon road. That's where I have to go to get the food. That's the only store that has the right brand of food."

"Okay, what kind of food?"

"It's called Happy Dog. I think it's their own brand. They got it in the back of the store by the ALLEY door. When you get to my house be careful Buffy doesn't BOWL you over when you go in. He's knocked me offa my PINS a couple a times before."

This did not sound a bit like the Sully I knew. She was emphasizing words and speaking in a funny, stilted tone and the Tidyman's she mentioned was closed. It was hard to hear her, too. There were occasional odd crashing noises that nearly drowned out her voice.

"Okay. I'll do that."

"Put the food in his blue BOWL or he won't eat."

Now that I knew that something was off. Buffy would eat anything, any-where, any time. He didn't care if his food was in a bowl or in a mud puddle. Then the light went on. Sully was trying to tell me where she was. She loved word games and was very good at them. I needed to think about what she said.

"Sully, are you...."

"That's enough," said a rough voice. "Do you have that quilt?"

"No, not yet," I said. "I just got home and I'm going to go look for it right now."

"Well, get a move on. You only got until tomorrow." The connection broke.

CHAPTER 33

▼

I sat and stared out the window. I knew Buffy wouldn't be hungry. He had an auto-dispense food dish on a timer. Every couple of hours it let out a serving of food. Sully had gotten it that so she would be free to leave with him in the house. If Buffy did not have food available he would eat the furniture. But, she learned the hard way that if she left a big bowl of food out he would eat it all at one time then throw up everywhere.

The food dispensing dish was her last hope. She said it took him only a day or two before he knew that food was coming steadily and she was able to safely leave him home by himself. I had seen it sitting in the kitchen the day I peeked in the window and the jar was full. Sully had told me that it held about a week's worth, so Buffy should be fine for a few days. He had a self-dispensing water dish that refilled itself, too, so I didn't have to waste any more time worrying about him. Besides which, I didn't have a key to Sully's house.

I closed my eyes, trying to concentrate. What was Sully trying to tell me? Again I nodded off and again awoke with a start. There was no noise in the house, but the crashing sounds in my head had awakened me. The sounds I was hearing were the ones from the long-closed Bowlero, where my dad loved to bowl. He had taken me with him on many occasions and that's where he taught me how to bowl. I got so I loved the sounds and smells of bowling lanes. Those noises were the same ones I had heard when I had talked to Norm earlier. I knew where Sully was.

The Tidyman's on McKinnon, in the Valley, Buffy bowling me over and knocking Sully off her pins, it was obvious.

"Valley Bowl, Henry, she's being held at Valley Bowl!"

I leaped to my feet and twirled around to grab my keys and felt a wave of dizziness. Blacks dots danced in front of my eyes. I dropped down into a chair and lowered my head until my vision cleared. What in the world was that all about? I looked at the clock, it was after seven. I hadn't eaten since noon; no wonder I nearly blacked out. My blood sugar was probably about 42. I stood up carefully and went into the kitchen.

I gulped down a peanut butter sandwich and a glass of milk, then started toward the door. I needed to go rescue Sully!

I got halfway out the door when I stopped again. Rick was on a farm call and I had no clue where he was. He would be mad if I went without him, but I had no idea when he would be back. He always turned his phone off on farms, too, the ring could spook an animal and a large spooked animal is dangerous. There was no point in leaving him a message, either, as he never checked those until he got home, so I would have to leave him a note and hope for the best. Then I looked down at my clothes. I was still wearing the khaki slacks and flowered shirt I had worn to work. Maybe something less visible would be wise. And, dumbbell, how about that .38? I ran to my bedroom.

Finally I was ready. Black jeans and a black zippered sweatshirt over a black T shirt would make me less visible when I was outside. The sweatshirt was one of the hooded kind with the big pockets in the front, perfect place to stash my little revolver. I left a note on the kitchen table for Rick and went to the door.

Henry was sitting on the little table by the door, looking expectant. He wanted to go along.

"Sorry, fella," I said, kissing his nose, "You need to stay here. How about getting that quilt out of its hidey hole while I'm gone, okay? If I can't find Sully tonight I'll need it for tomorrow."

CHAPTER 34

▼

It was a league night at Valley Bowl and the place was hopping. I couldn't imagine where Sully might be, certainly not out in the front in plain view, I wouldn't think. I went in and wandered about, but saw no sign of either her or the vile Norm. She must be someplace in the back part of the building.

The trouble was, there was really no back to this building, just the pin setting equipment. There must be some kind of space behind them where Sully is being held. I needed to get back behind the electric pin setters, but how? I knew that one way would be to walk down one of the narrow aisles that ran along the outside of the lanes on the far left and right sides of the building, but I also knew that customers were not allowed in that area and that I would be stopped. But, it seemed it was the only way to get to the back part of the building.

I sat down and watched the bowlers for a few minutes, trying to decide what to do. Should I try and hide someplace until closing time, then look around? There was probably a security system, though. I needed to find out. I went up to the desk and got some quarters for a pull tab machine. Sure enough, I was able to spot the alarm keypad. There was a row of lights over the number keys and each one flashed green. Of course the place would have an alarm, with the pull tabs and other gambling items that could be stolen, not to mention all the alcohol behind the bar. I would have to leave when everybody else did.

I sat back down and opened my pull tabs. Golly, all losers. What a surprise. I was feeling like a real loser myself. I stared down the lane in front of me, watching a bowler's big curve ball mow down the pins. I could see the automatic pin setter shuffling the pins into position and then putting them in the rack that would set them back down. As the rack lowered, I caught a flash of light behind them. Where had that come from?

I watched the next cycle. There was light behind the pinsetters, but it was faint and yellow. That had been a brighter flash, almost a blue-white color, it looked like the same kind of light from the quartz iodide street lights outside the townhouse in Seattle.

Of course! That flash of light had come in from the parking lot, probably through an open back door.

I jumped to my feet, then grabbed my gun just before it bounced out of my pocket. That would be all I would need about now, to attract a bunch of attention. I stretched and sighed, then sauntered out the door, wanting to run the whole way.

Once outside, the saunter became a dash. I ran around the corner of the building and sure enough, there was a door in the back of the building. It was propped open with an old coffee can full of cigarette butts. Moving slower now, I went up to the door and peeked inside.

A string of bare overhead bulbs cast a yellowish glow. The noise was almost deafening and I wished I had my shooters ear protection with me. I could see a young-looking man at the far end of the hallway. I stepped inside, momentarily blocking the light from outside. I stepped all the way inside and stepped out of the light and this time I caught the man's attention. He looked up with a frown. I smiled and beckoned to him.

I stepped back outside and he came out, pulling ear plugs out as he came through the door.

"What do you want back here?" he said, scowling.

"I just wondered if you could give me a quick tour. I have always wanted to watch you guys do your thing with the pins; it looks fascinating." I opened my eyes as wide as I could and tried to look impressed. "The machinery looks SO complicated."

The young man tugged at his ratty T-shirt, smoothing it across his meager chest. "Yeah," he said, "It is a pretty involved job. I guess it would be okay if I showed you around."

"Oh, goody," I said, "I would just LOVE that."

I stuffed some wads of Kleenex in my ears and stepped into the back of the bowling alley. If Sully were being held here, she'd be deaf soon.

I was glad the young man was not able to talk to me. I didn't have to try and maintain a pretense of interest, but could look around.

There was no place that Sully, or anybody, could be hiding. The area behind the bowling alleys was just big enough to hold the huge pinsetting machines with a narrow walkway behind them. They are fascinating to watch and I really wished I could spend the evening. The young man just had to make sure no pins got caught in a place where they would jam the pinsetters. While I watched, he had to step out onto one alley and retrieve a pin that had bounced too far away from the bar that swept the fallen pins back in the pit at the end of the alley where the pinsetter scooped them up. But, except for a tiny room containing a toilet and a sink, and other with a small table and couple of chairs, there was no room for anything else. Norm may have called me from Valley Bowl, but Sully was not here.

I stepped out the door, the young man following me.

"Thank you so much," I gushed. "I always wanted to see what it was like back here. Thanks again!"

He started to say something, then shrugged and pulled out a cigarette. "No problem," he said.

I went back to the Blazer and sat down. My ears were glad to be rid of their crude noise blockers, but they still rang from the decibel level in the back of the bowling lanes. But, where was Sully?

I needed to go look around behind the building some more, but I didn't want to risk being seen by the pinsetter. I looked at the clock on the dash, it was nearly ten o'clock. The league bowling should be done pretty soon, then maybe he would leave. I scrunched down in the seat to wait.

Time crept. My neck was getting stiff and I was beginning to get cold before the first of the bowlers trickled out the door. Soon there was a rush of people and the parking lot emptied. I glanced over to the auto repair shop next door to Valley Bowl. If I moved the Blazer over there it would be less conspicuous.

From my new spot I could watch the back of the building where I had gone in to look for Sully. Within moments of the last of the bowlers leaving, I saw my pinsetter guy come out the back door. He locked it and shook the knob to make sure it was secure. Then he climbed into a small, rusty car and drove away. I sat for a few more minutes thinking about what to do next. The lounge would be open for awhile longer, but those peoples' cars were parked in the front. With bowling over for the night I should be able to look around undetected out in the back and wouldn't be seen by the people in the bar even if they came out to their cars. I turned out the dome light so the Blazer would stay dark when I opened the door. I slid out and started to ease the door shut.

CHAPTER 35

▼

"What in the hell are you doing?"

I gasped and would have fallen but for the hand that clutched my arm. Before I could react I felt arms wrap around me and I was picked up nearly off my feet. "Are you trying to get yourself killed?"

"Oh, my God, Rick, you are scaring the shit out of me. Put me down!"

Rick let go of me as quickly as he had grabbed me. He stood in front of me, fists clenched and eyes flashing.

"I got home and found your note. What in the world do you think you are doing? Why didn't you call the cops like I told you to?"

"Sssssssh. Calm down and let me tell you what happened. You were gone today on your farm calls when Sully came into the clinic. I assume it's that Norm maniac who grabbed her and put a pipe bomb on her. He said he would set it off if anything funny happened.

"Then, after I got home she called me with a weird message about feeding Buffy. She was able to tell me that she was here, at Valley Bowl. She isn't though, at least not inside the building. I was afraid if I called the police they would come in like gangbusters and Norm would set off the bomb. I want to try and find her first, then call them when I know where she is."

Rick stood and glared at me. "Can you imagine how I felt when I got home and found your note? Why couldn't you at least wait for me to come with you?"

"Because I never know now late you were going to be on farm call days. Norm expects me to have that quilt for him by morning and I still can't find it." The tears I was fighting started to fall. I was worried sick about Sully and now Rick was mad at me. "Tonight might be the only chance to save Sully's life. I have to try." I sagged back into the Blazer and reached for Kleenex. Rick crouched down by the open door.

"I'm sorry, Maggie. But, damn it, you take too many risks. Let's go call the cops, right now."

"Rick, please, not quite yet. Can we just look around behind the bowling alley first? I know I could hear pinsetters in the background when Norm called me, and Sully all but told me she was here. Please, let's just look around for a few minutes."

Rick glowered at me. "This is totally against my better judgment," he said, "But I guess it wouldn't hurt to just LOOK."

I blew my nose one last time. "I was just getting ready to go around the outside of the back of the building. I was able to get in behind the pinsetting machines earlier. I asked the guy tending them for a tour and he was happy to oblige, but Sully wasn't there. There also were no places where she could be kept, either. So, I figure there has to be a place separate from the bowling building itself."

Rick and I walked across the car lot to the back of Valley Bowl. I saw Rick's pickup parked out by the street—that was how he was able to sneak up on me. I would have to develop my observation skills if I was going to continue to try and play detective.

There were several storage sheds behind Valley Bowl, all of them securely locked. Two of them were solid on all sides, but the others had small windows. I didn't see any cars back here, either. Norm might not be around, even if Sully was being held in one of the buildings.

"Do you have a flashlight in the truck, Rick?"

"Yeah, wait here. I'll go get it."

I stood and listened, but other than the cars going by on Sprague, all was quiet. If Sully was in one of these buildings she might be alone. I shivered, wishing I were home in bed rolled up in a quilt.

"Let's see if we can see in any of these buildings," I said when Rick came back with the flashlight.

"It's a good thing we're both tall," he muttered. He still did not look very happy, but he was less angry, anyway.

Before we tried peeking in windows, Rick used his flashlight to tap on the doors of the solid wood buildings. There was no response. We went up to the first building with a window.

After a few tries, we discovered if we held the flashlight right up against the glass we could get some light to go into the building. Our look in this first building showed us nothing but discarded equipment and dirt. But, in the next building I could see a table in the middle of the floor and what looked like a cot against the far wall. It seemed like there was something on the cot, too, but I couldn't tell if it was a person or just a pile of junk. We tapped on the door, but the bundle did not stir.

"We need to get in there," I said. "That might be Sully; she might be hurt."

"Now it's time to get some help, Maggie. We can't just go busting into somebody's else's property."

"But, Rick, the police won't want to break in there either. It will take forever to get them convinced that something is going on; they won't be very happy with us."

"Well, I'm not very happy with us, either." Rick sighed. "I think I have a bolt cutter in the truck, let me go look."

While he walked back to his truck I stood on my tiptoes and looked in the window. The bundle on the cot looked like it was in a slightly different position. This just had to be Sully. I walked to the door and looked at the lock. It was a combination lock, similar to the one I used at Stroh's. Frustrated, I reached out and gave it a yank.

CHAPTER 36

▼

The lock dropped open. Stunned, I stared at it. Then, with fingers suddenly nerveless, I pulled it out of the hasp.

"Okay, Maggie …"

"Wait, Rick, the lock opened, look!"

"How did you …"

"I didn't, not really. My lock at Stroh's does this sometimes if I don't push it together firmly enough. It looks like it's closed, but it's not, especially if you don't turn the dial away from the last number when you close it. I just tugged on this one and it popped open."

"Well, we might as well go in as long as we've done this much." Rick pulled the door open and we stepped inside.

The little room smelled like an outhouse. I saw the full chamber pot by the foot of the bed and knew why. A tiny electric space heater put out a feeble whisper of warmth. There were empty fast food containers on the table and I saw a pair of familiar-looking shoes. I went over to the cot and pulled the blankets away from the mound there. It was a person. I bent closer, yes, it was Sully. I could see her chest move; she was alive.

"Sully, it's Maggie, wake up, Sully."

"Wha?? Wha's that?"

Sully's eyes opened, but the pupils were tiny and seemed to look right through me.

"Sully, it's me, Maggie. Are you all right?" I pulled her shirt up and the pipe bomb was no longer there. I looked around. On the floor was a piece of pipe with some duct tape and dangling wires hanging from it. That must be the bomb. We had to get out of there.

Sully's mouth hung open. She licked her lips and tried to sit up.

"Wha? Don't touch ... Let me ..." she slurred and tried to swing her arm in what seemed like an attempt to hit me. She had no idea who I was or what was going on.

"Rick, we'll have to carry her. She's been drugged."

"Yeah, I can see that," he said. "Okay, Sully, let's go."

Like she weighed no more than a sack of grain, Rick hoisted Sully over his shoulder. She beat her fists again his back in a futile attempt to get him to put her down.

"Let's get out of here," he said. "Lock the door behind us."

"I have a quilt in the back of the Blazer, put her on the back seat and cover her up," I said. "I'll be right there." I grabbed Sully's shoes and looked around to see if there was anything else of hers in the shed. There was nothing. I closed the door behind me and made sure the lock was securely fastened.

By the time I got back to the Blazer Sully was sleeping in the back seat. Rick pulled his truck up next to me. "Shouldn't we take Sully to the ER?"

"No, I think she will be okay. She acts like she just got a big dose of a sedative. Let's take her home and see how she does. This might be a bit hard to explain at the hospital."

"Okay. I'll see you at home." Rick pulled his truck out of the parking lot. He was still being a bit short with me, but no longer seemed quite so angry. I hoped he would able to deal with my impulsive nature, because I didn't think I could change it much.

I sat in the Blazer for a minute, waiting for my heart rate to slow down. In spite of having been in danger in the past, I still was rattled by the evening's events. I turned the key and the engine caught. Heat would be good, too. I turned the heater up full blast and pulled out onto Sprague. I would have to go west for a couple of blocks to find a cross street back to east-bound Appleway. Sprague Avenue was one way west until it got to Fancher Road.

A rusty blue car suddenly lurched in front of me, nearly hitting my front fender. With a jolt I recognized it, this was the same car Norm had driven on the night he had come to my house. I saw him glare at me through the window, then lurch his car toward me again.

Rick was nowhere to be seen; he had too much of a head start to be of any help. I fumbled for my cell phone as I slammed on the brakes, just missing a collision with Norm. I jerked the steering wheel to the left and swerved around him. I gave up on the cell phone, this was going to take both hands.

I floored the gas and blasted away from Norm. I could hear what sounded like backfires coming from behind me, then a slamming noise from the back end of the Blazer. Oh, my God, he was shooting at me. Another car came up beside me and as they passed me I saw the back window shatter. Norm must have fired again. The car ran off the side of the road and lurched to a stop. I felt another bullet hit the Blazer.

While my attention was distracted by what was happening next to me, Norm had caught up. This was not good. I saw his headlights in the mirror and heard a crunching noise at the same time that my head slammed back into the head rest. Norm had run into the back end of the Blazer. I flew by an intersection just as Norm fired again. I jerked the wheel to the left and my tires squealed as I changed lanes.

Norm was still behind me. What was I going to do? If I could just make it to a convenience store, a bar, anywhere where there people who could help before his aim improved. I floored the accelerator and ducked down as low as I could and still be able to see out.

Another intersection was just ahead. With a screech that made me fear losing my tires, I made a left turn and then left again, zooming out onto Appleway. At least I was heading in the right direction now.

I peeked into the side mirror. Norm had made the turns right behind me, but he stopped shooting and his car was swerving back and forth across Appleway. Now he was the one being pursued. I didn't know who it was, either the State Patrol or the Sheriff, but it was two cars' worth. Those flashing red and blue lights were the prettiest thing I had seen in a long time. I zipped into a parking lot and stopped behind a dump truck that was parked there. Norm flew by me, the police in hot pursuit, the scream of their sirens splitting the night quiet.

I pulled back out on the street. I could see the flashing lights moving fast away from me and the siren wails faded. I followed, wanting to see Norm caught. Plus, I had a story to tell the patrolmen.

CHAPTER 37

▼

I didn't get the chance. I was almost close enough to hear the screaming sirens again when a huge cloud of dust erupted in the distance. The flashing lights stopped moving away from me and the sirens stopped in mid shriek. The police must have stopped Norm.

By the time I got up to the police cars, the dust was blowing away. Norm had tried to make a turn, but failed. His rusty old car was folded around a power pole. I couldn't imagine how he could have survived such an impact. Sully was now groaning in the back seat. The drugs must be wearing off. I knew I needed to talk to the police, but now there was no rush. I decided to take Sully home. I would call Marty the first thing in the morning. I made a sedate turn onto Mullan Road and headed north.

Rick had opened up the Murphy bed in my office and it was ready for Sully. She was now able to walk on her own, but fell asleep the minute we helped her into bed. I propped her up on a stack of pillows so she wouldn't be at risk to lose her airway while she slept, then wobbled my way out to the kitchen.

Rick was standing at the stove, stirring hot cocoa. "You look like you could use this," he said, handing me a cup. "I was just about to go back and look for you. What took you so long to get home?"

It took every bit of concentration I had to sit down at the table without falling. "Norm showed up, he shot at me, then crashed …"

"WHAT!" shouted Rick, "When did this happen?"

I picked up the cup and took a long swallow. I could feel the heat clear down into my toes and I swear I could feel the sugar going right into my brain cells. I could actually think by the time the cup was half empty. "More, please," I said.

Rick obliged, but nearly slopped the cocoa out onto the table, his hands were shaking so. "Will you PLEASE tell me what happened," he said.

"Well, I sat for a minute after you left to gather my wits. Then, just as I pulled out onto Sprague Norm showed up. He started to chase me and he was shooting at me. I think he hit the rear door of the Blazer at least twice and he ran into me, too. Another car got in the way and he shot out their back window. I hope they are okay. I should call ..." I got up to get the phone.

"Finish telling me what happened first," Rick said.

I sat back down. "Well, I just kept going as fast as I could, swerving back and forth to try and keep out of his range. There must have been policemen on a side street, 'cause all of a sudden they were chasing Norm. I pulled over and let them go by. The next think I knew I saw a big cloud of dust. I drove up to look and Norm had crashed into a power pole. I knew I should stop and tell the patrolmen what happened, but I wanted to get Sully home. I can't call them now; I can't even think straight. I'll call them in the morning."

"My, God, Maggie, I should have stayed and followed you home. You could have been killed." Tears stood in Rick's eyes.

"Please, take me to bed," I sobbed. "I am done in."

He must have done as I asked, because the next thing I knew it was morning.

CHAPTER 38

▼

The coffee smelled wonderful and I could hear sizzling noises. Somebody was cooking. I lurched out of bed, noting that I was still wearing my black skulking outfit of the night before.

Sully was standing at my stove, her five-foot, hundred-pound body nearly lost in one of my bib aprons. She was stirring scrambled eggs with one hand and pulling toast out of the toaster with the other.

"Rick said for you to take the day off," she said. "Have a sit-down; breakfast will be ready in a jiffy."

I stared at Sully. Under the apron she was wearing a set of my sweats, the pant legs rolled up so they wouldn't drag on the floor. She looked like she had just come back from a delightful, restful, vacation. A glance in the hall mirror had shown me to look like a train wreck. My dark hair was short, but still managed to stick out in fifty-seven different directions and the dark circles under my eyes seem to run down to my jaw. My eyes were bloodshot and my mouth tasted like the north end of a southbound camel. I peeled my lips apart and poured coffee in.

Sully slid a plate of food in front of me. "Eat, eat," she said. "I already had mine."

"Thank you," I said weakly. "You obviously are okay this morning."

"Slept like a baby," she said, her cackle of laughter filling the kitchen. "Lot better than I did the night before, though, I gotta tell ya."

"I am so out of the loop on this, Sully. You need to tell me what happened."

"Well, nothing much. That creep, said his name was Norm, just came to my door with a big gun in his hand. If I'da knowed what he was up to I'da shot him first. But, I answered the door empty handed. Pretty dumb. I won't do that again. He made me get in his car and he took me to that shed."

"And then he called me and brought you to the clinic the next day with that bomb on you," I said. "I was scared to death."

"I was a bit scared, too, Maggie, that's for sure. But, after we got back to the shed he took it off. He said it wouldn't matter, I would still be a goner if he set it off. It's still there somewhere, I guess. He gave me some kind of drugs in a cup of coffee, really put me out. Every time I would wake up he would let me use the commode then he would give me some more drugs. Next thing I knowed I was here."

I told Sully my part of what happened the night before. "Now, I need to call the police and tell them what happened. I also want to know what happened to the car Norm shot at and if the people in it are okay. I better do that now. Thanks for cooking for me, Sully, you saved my life."

"Well, I owed you," she said.

I was glad Rick gave me the day off. I called the Sheriff's office and before I could say more than three words they told me a car was coming to pick up me and Sully. Her statement only took a short time, but I spent most of the rest of the day sitting with various deputies and detectives.

"His name was Norm Seeber," one deputy told me. "He did not survive the collision with the power pole. Why was he chasing you?"

I told them the story about Norm showing up my house, demanding the quilt that Phil told him to come and get. I told them about Barbara Hughes and everything that I knew about that.

"My cat has somehow managed to hide that quilt. I knew if that I couldn't produce it Norm would kill Sully. He let her call me with a message about feeding her dog and she was able to give me enough clues so I could figure out where she was. I went and found her and when I went to leave with her that's when he started chasing us. I haven't had a chance to look yet, but I think there are a couple of bullet holes in my rear door. He shot at another car and hit their window. Are those people okay?"

"Yes," said the deputy, "They were lucky. All that the bullet hit was the back window and then went out the side window."

"Did Sully tell you about the bomb?"

All the men sitting in the office with me straightened up. "Bomb?" one of them said.

"Yes. Norm fastened a pipe bomb to her when she came to get the quilt the first time. She said he left it in that shed and I saw something that looked like a pipe bomb when I took her out of there."

One deputy jumped up and grabbed a phone and starting talking fast into it. "... so don't start digging around in there until we can get the bomb squad out," he said.

"I guess Sully forgot that part," he said. "Thanks for letting us know."

"So, Sully was with you last night?" asked another deputy.

"Yes, that's why I didn't stop when I saw the crash. She had been drugged and I wanted to get her home."

The deputy nodded. "Okay, that makes some sense. If you ever get into a situation like this again, though, you need to call us before going off on your own."

I nodded. There was really no reply I could make to that.

"Now, the question we all have is this," said a different deputy, "What is so important about that quilt?"

"I have no idea," I said, "And, I can't even find the stupid thing. It's really ugly, all sorts of fabrics and colors, and covered with knots. I can't imagine why Barbara made it in the first place."

"Well, let us know when you find it," the deputy said. "We will need to take a look at it."

CHAPTER 39

▼

By the time the deputy dropped me off at home Rick was there and dinner was cooking. It was wonderful to just go inside and collapse.

"First breakfast cooked for me and now dinner. You and Sully are going to spoil me," I said, pushing myself away from the table. "That was wonderful."

"Well, I have to eat, too," Rick said. "Now, in the future, please don't go off on any of these expeditions without me along, okay?"

"Okay, but that means you'll have to tell me where you are going to be, and promise to check your messages before the end of the day."

"Deal," he said. "That quilt is still missing?"

"Yes. I can't believe Henry hasn't drug it back out of whatever hidey hole he found for it. I have searched everywhere."

"It will show up eventually."

"I wish that would be sooner rather than later. I am really curious to know what could be so important about it."

Rick was still upset with me. He would have to either accept me as I was or we would have no future. I was not going to stop helping my friends if they needed me, even if I did have to be the fool that rushes in where angels fear to tread.

We just settled down to watch a movie when Rose showed up at the door.

Rick sighed and got up to let his mother in. "Hi, mom. How are you?"

"Hello, Rick. I'm fine. I just wanted to come by and see you for a few minutes. Do you have any coffee?"

With a sigh of my own I got up and got her a cup. Rick turned off the TV, the movie would have to wait.

"Well, Maggie, I won't stay long," Rose said, sipping daintily at her coffee. "I just wanted you to know that today I joined a women's auxiliary from the Lutheran church. I won't be able to come over and keep you occupied as much as I have been. I am going to be working with the auxiliary on several of their volunteer projects. I do have a request, though."

Hoping my relief wasn't showing on my face, I said, "That's great, Rose! You need to get to know people around here."

"Yes. I was getting a little lonely. Anyway, what I wanted to ask you is if you would make me a quilt? Just a small one, to put over my legs when I'm sitting watching TV. It is so much chillier here in the fall than it is in Florida."

"Funny you would mention that, Rose, I already have one in mind for you. Would you like to see the fabric I picked out for you and the pattern?"

"Oh, what fun! No, I would rather be surprised. I just have one request: Could you make it look different? I like things that are a little unusual."

"Yes. I can do that," I said. "I found a really special piece of fabric that I didn't want to have to cut up and I have an idea for it. Plus, it will be a little faster to make, so you won't have to be chilly for too long."

"Don't rush, Maggie. I have a blanket I'm using now, but I will love having a special quilt. I won't linger tonight. I'll see you in few days, Rick."

Almost before we could react, she was up and out the door.

"That was interesting," I said.

Rick nodded, looking slightly cynical. "I know what she is up to," he said. "She will be having this women's group coming to her place and she wants to be able to impress them. Having a custom-made quilt will be a place to start."

I couldn't help but laugh. "Oh, isn't it fun to be used! I might get some quilt orders from the ladies in the group, too, so I could benefit. You know, though, what I really like about your mother? She may be a bit of a prima donna and all that, but she is kind. My mother thinks she hot stuff, too, only she can be nasty. I can't imagine your mom being mean or anything like that."

"That's true. I don't think my mother has a mean bone in her body. She can just be so annoying at times."

"I sort of figured that out, too. She is like a toddler, you have to attend to her at every moment."

"What, you mean watch her so she doesn't run into the street?" Rick was laughing now.

"No, I just mean that you have to pay attention; she expects appropriate responses to everything she says, and she says a lot."

Rick nodded and pulled me close. He turned the TV back on and we settled in to watch the rest of the movie.

CHAPTER 40

▼

The black flannel fabric with the rose bouquets on it would be perfect for Rick's mom's quilt. I would cut out star shapes in the flannel and place a piece of plain colored flannel behind the hole. Then, I would turn the edge of the top flannel under and hand stitch it in place. This is called reverse appliqué and gives a unique look, as apposed to cutting out stars of the plain flannel and appliquéing them on the top of the fabric. Then, all I would have to do was add a border or two and quilt it.

I found two wonderful flannels, an olivey green and a honey-gold to use for the stars. I decided to have olivey green stars, in three different sizes, cluster up in the top left corner then flow down the side and curve around and across the bottom of the quilt where honey-gold stars would cluster in the bottom right corner. A name for this quilt almost presented itself: Starring Rose. I set aside enough of each flannel fabric to make the stars then cut 2 1/2" strips from the what was left. I cut these into pieces of various lengths and sewed them together end-to-end at a 45 degree angle until I had a strip long enough to go twice around the center piece of the quilt. This made a double border around the center of the quilt. The top I would finish off with a border of plain black. I would use a piece of the floral to make the binding. I looked at my sketch. This really would be an unusual quilt.

With the main piece cut out for the center of the quilt, I made three star patterns out of cardboard. I chose which bouquets to cut out and put a safety pin on each place where I would put a star. I cut squares of the green and honey-gold fabrics and traced the shape of the star on the back of those squares using my cardboard patterns. Then, I placed those squares under the previously chosen bouquet areas of the rose fabric. I made sure the right side of the green and gold fabric was facing the wrong side of the big piece of rose covered fabric. I pinned the squares in place. Working from the back I stitched on my drawn star lines, using a bright yellow thread in the bobbin that would show up against the black bouquet fabric.

After I stitched all the pieces of fabric for the stars in place, I turned the top over so that I was looking at the front. Being careful not to cut through the square of fabric on the back, I cut away the black/rose fabric about one quarter inch from the yellow stitching. The raw edge of the black fabric I turned under about three sixteenths of an inch and hand stitched it to the star fabric. Once each star was done, I pulled out the yellow guide stitching. Now some of the rose bouquets were replaced with a star shining through from behind.

I was pleased with how this method was working out; it was a new one for me. Rose would certainly have a unique quilt to show off.

CHAPTER 41

▼

"So what do you think?" I held the quilt I had named Starring Rose up for approval or rejection. I quilted it rather simply, just did a wandering stipple in the black outer border, and then stitched around each star and bouquet in the center. I did a more-complex design in the double honey-gold and green border, which really set it off. I held my breath.

Rose tipped her head from side to side, considering. "It's perfect," she finally said. "I have never seen anything like this and I bet nobody else has, either. Wherever did you find the pattern?"

"It's my original design, Rose. Take a look at the label," I said, turning the corner of the quilt back. "See, it says so right here."

Her face pinked as she read the Starring Rose title. "This is just wonderful," she said, beaming.

Whew. I allowed myself to breathe. I passed the test; she liked the quilt.

"Now, let's have dinner," Rick said.

"So Bob, Tony, Jerry and I are going to be going to the gulf coast in ten days. We will stay for at least a month, but it could be longer if they still need help at the end of that time. Bob was able to get us open-end return tickets," Rick said, passing the green beans to his mother.

"It's so good of you boys to do this," Rose said. "Maggie and I will just have to bumble along without you." She smiled at me.

I hoped my smile did not look as sickly as it felt.

Rose toddled off to her car, stuffed with ham and clutching her quilt. Rick waved good-bye and turned to me. But before he could open his mouth, the phone rang. He bared his teeth at me in a semblance of a smile. I knew he did not want to be called out again tonight.

"It's for you," he said, looking relieved.

"Hello?" I listened for a minute, then my knees buckled. Thank goodness I was near a chair. "Okay," I said, "I'll try."

I dropped the phone and stared at Rick. "It's not over," I managed to whisper.

"What? What's not over? What are you talking about, Maggie?"

"That was some guy named Stub. He said just because Norm was dead that didn't mean that Phil was giving up on getting his quilt."

"You still haven't found that thing, have you? What else did he say?"

"Nothing much, just that I would be hearing from him again. Oh, Rick, what are we going to do? I wish I could figure out what was so important about that quilt."

Rick picked up the phone. "That's the last straw, Maggie. I'm calling Marty."

"I agree. I don't want to have to rescue anybody or myself again." I sat and listened to Rick leave a message on Marty's voice mail. While he talked, I pondered. Suddenly I had the sensation of a light bulb going on over my head.

I leaped to my feet. "Hey! I bet I know where that quilt is! You know how the bed sits on that platform? Remember the little door the store put in the front part, so that there was a storage area between the two boxes that support the mattress? I never put anything in there, it's too hard to get it back out. That's the only place in the whole house, short of the toilet tank in the downstairs bathroom, that I haven't searched. Let's go!"

Before Rick could even get to his feet I was in the bedroom lying flat on the floor. There were actually two little doors over the opening between the support boxes for the mattress platform. There were no handles, there was just a scooped out area on the bottom edge of the door, ideal for a black paw. I pulled the doors open.

"Here's a flashlight. Can you see anything?" Rick was lying at the foot of the bed, peering over the edge of the mattress at me.

"Yes! There it is, but I can't reach it. Hand me my backscratcher, will you?"

"I'll never again give you a hard time about having backscratchers all over the place," said Rick, as I pulled Barbara's ugly quilt out of its hiding place. "Now, let's take a good look at that thing."

We went into the dining room and spread the quilt out on the table. We studied the top, but saw nothing but wild colors and French knots. We turned it over, but the back was just a plain piece of fabric. Nothing to see there, either. I picked up the quilt and started running it through my hands.

The binding was lumpy in one spot and crinkled when I squeezed it. "Grab me my orange scissors off the table by my chair, would you, Rick?"

It only took a few snips to loosen the stitching holding the binding in place and then I was unfolding a tiny piece of paper. "What in the world …" I moved the paper over under the lamp to read the tiny writing. 'The key is in the quilt,' it said.

"The key is in the quilt, the key is in the quilt," Rick muttered. "What does that mean?"

"I don't know," I said. "Maybe there is something written inside the binding. I don't see anything on the back or the front. Let me take the rest of the stitches out."

Barbara had done a good job hand sewing the edge of the binding to the back. Even though this was an ugly quilt, she had put her best effort into finishing it. I snipped along, stopping every now and then to examine the inside of the binding. There were only a couple of inches of binding left to take out and I had seen nothing. I turned the quilt to make it easier to work on and something slid down my leg and clinked on the floor. Rick leaned down and picked it up.

"What's this?" said Rick, holding up a small piece of metal. "It looks like a key."

"It is, Rick, she meant it literally: THE KEY IS IN THE QUILT. We found it!"

"Yes, we did. But, what it is a key for? It doesn't look like a door key."

"No, it doesn't. Hmmm. You know what, I bet this is the key to the place where Phil hid his embezzled money. Barbara told me that money he took from Home Improvement, Inc. had never been recovered. She told me that he had given her a large amount of money to keep secure for him, and I bet that was it. She must have told him that the location of the hiding place for the money is in this quilt. No wonder he is so desperate to get a hold of it."

"Well, that's about enough excitement for me for one day," said Rick. "Let's get some sleep. You can give that key to Marty tomorrow."

"I will, but first I think I'll stop by Gary's Key and Lock in Millwood and see what he can tell me about it. It'd be fun to be able to lead Marty to the money."

CHAPTER 42

▼

"Good morning, Gary's Key and Lock." Good, Mary, Gary's wife, answered the phone and they were open.

"Hi, Mary, this is Maggie Jackson. I'm glad you are there. Is Gary around or did he get called out?"

"Hi, Maggie. No, Gary's here. What's up"

"I have an odd key I need to show him. I'll be down in a few minutes."

I could hardly get out the door fast enough. Marty called me earlier and asked me to come to his office. I knew he was expecting me shortly, but I had to find out whatever I could about this key.

"It's a safety deposit box key," said Gary, turning the key over in his hand.

"Is there any way to tell where it comes from?" I asked.

"No, unfortunately not. These keys are deliberately not marked, so if one is lost or stolen the wrong person couldn't try to access the box. The only thing I can tell about it is that is from here in the U.S. versus an overseas bank or whatever. I have no idea where it came from though, could be anywhere in the country."

"Rats. Well, thanks anyway, Gary. This is a crime-related key, so I'm going to drop it at the Sheriff's office today."

"… and the key was hidden in the binding of the quilt," I told Marty. "But, on my way here I stopped at Gary at Gary's Key and Lock and he said there's no way to tell what it unlocks, other than it is a safety deposit box key."

"Yeah," said Marty, "I've seen them before; I recognized it."

"How will you go about figuring out where it's from, anyway?"

"I suppose I'll take a trip to Walla Walla and see if I can get Phil to tell me."

"You think he knows? This is the key to the money, but it doesn't really tell where the money is."

Marty shrugged. "I don't know. Phil may know where the key belongs. It would help at his parole hearing if he made restitution of the money, that's for sure. At least we now know why he is so desperate to get that quilt, anyway."

"If it will help him I hope he doesn't tell you," I said. "I would like to see him rot in jail forever."

"In the meantime, we need to do something about this Stub character that called you. He didn't give a last name?"

"No, just said that I'd be hearing from him. Should I give him the quilt now that we have the key?"

Marty frowned over steepled fingers. "Do you know if Phil knows what this quilt Barbara made looks like?"

I shrugged. "I have no idea. I certainly have not been in contact with him."

"There may be something more to this quilt, something we haven't figured out. Does there seem to be any message of any sort on it? Like a bank name and address?" Marty laughed at himself. "Sounds pretty far-fetched, huh?"

I shook my head. "Not really, not if you knew how devious Phil could be. I have an idea. Why don't I throw together some kind of ugly quilt. I have a bunch of scraps I could use up. Then, when this Stub character calls back, I will have something to give him. You could follow him after he has it, although I bet he goes straight to the state prison to see Phil. I would love to put a message on the top, like 'fuck you, Phil,' or something along those lines."

"I didn't know you could talk like that, Maggie," now Marty was laughing at me.

"I've heard the word before and it seems appropriate. So, what do you think? Should I make an ugly quilt?"

"That might just work, Maggie. Go ahead and do that, then call me the minute you hear from this Stub guy again. Did his number show up on your called ID, by the way?"

"No, it was blocked. He was at least smart enough to do that. Okay, Marty, I'll go home and toss something together. This will be an interesting project."

CHAPTER 43

▼

I had seen crazy quilts before, but I had never made one. There had never been a reason to and I didn't particularly like them. In the 1920's, women made them and used them as home décor. They usually did not have a batting, so they weren't really quilts per the definition, which is two layers of cloth with a filling of some sort between them that are all sewn together. But, these crazy quilts were made to be tossed over the back of a sofa, as decoration on a piano, or even used as a tablecloth. They were often elaborately embroidered on the top, also.

A crazy quilt of this type is made somewhat randomly. The maker figured out what size she wanted the quilt to be and then cut out squares of plain muslin usually about six to eight inches in size. These squares served as a foundation for the scraps. Once enough squares had been cut out to make a quilt the desired size the construction began.

The first scrap is laid face up in place on the muslin, making sure it extends past at least one edge of the muslin. Then, another scrap is laid face down on top of the first scrap with at least one edge lined up with the edge of the bottom fabric. A seam is sewn along this matching edge of the fabric. If necessary, the seam allowance is trimmed to about 1/4". The fabric that had just been sewn down is opened out and pressed face up in place along the seam line. More pieces are added of all shapes and sizes, following the same steps each time, put a piece face down over the previously placed piece, seam, trim, fold out the piece, and press. This is done until the muslin square is completely covered. The square is then turned over and the edges of the various fabrics are trimmed even with the muslin square.

Once enough squares are assembled, they are arranged in strips, sewn together, then the strips are sewn together. Some quilters would then spend hours doing a fancy embroidery stitch, often using yarn, over all the seams, or embroider fancy things in the fabric patches themselves. Then, they sewed the back to the front at the seam lines between the blocks to hold the back in place. A binding was applied, just like for a regular quilt.

I wouldn't go to that much work. I didn't ever want to give Phil anything, but this was for a good purpose. I had an old sheet I used for rags and I cut out enough squares to make a baby size quilt, about 36 by 44 inches. I pulled out my bag of large scraps that I save from all my projects and got busy.

Because I was just slap-dashing this together, it took me no time at all to make the top. I threaded my longarm machine with monofilament thread (fishing line to the non quilter!) and fastened the back in place. I took a short cut with the binding, just made the back piece big enough so that I could fold over the edge and machine stitch it to the top. I was not the least bit careful of puckers and lumps and did not really care how it looked. I even remembered to put the 'To Phil From Barbara' message along the binding seam on the back. It was almost fun, sewing like this.

I would spend a few minutes adding some French knots to the top, in case Phil knew they would be there. That I could do after dinner while I watched the news.

"Oh, that's nice," said Rick, looking confused. "Who is that for?"

I had to laugh at his expression. He was trying so hard to be diplomatic, after all, I HAD made this thing.

"It's a decoy. Marty said that if I had something to give to this guy Stub when he shows up it could buy some us some time. Marty said they will follow him and if he goes to see Phil then maybe they could learn where the money is. I'm going to fancy it up with some French knots, too."

"That will help a lot." Now Rick was laughing, too. "Whew. I'm glad I don't have to pretend I like that thing, it is pretty ugly."

CHAPTER 44

▼

The next morning when Stub called me at the clinic I was ready. My fingers were sore from making French knots, but I had a nice lumpy quilt for him. As soon as I disconnected the call from Stub I called the sheriff's office.

"So, Marty, he told me to leave it in the back of the Blazer and he would come by the clinic and get it. But, I have no idea when."

"I'm coming right over," he said. "I have a tiny locator we can put in it and then we can track it without Stub getting suspicious."

Within minutes Marty was in the door. "Can you hide this somewhere?" he asked, handing me what looked almost like a foil button.

I had to use suture material to sew up the spot I picked open, but I was able to slip the small coin-shaped tracking device into one of the lumpier spots in the binding around the crazy quilt. It didn't show at all.

The quilt went into the back seat of the Blazer. I wanted to spend the rest of the day watching it, but clients and their pets just kept coming in. When I went out and looked at lunchtime the quilt was gone. Stub had snuck in and gotten it without my noticing. But, at least he had it and I was safe again for the time being.

It was five minutes before five. I was just reaching out to switch the phone over to the answering service when it rang under my hand. I jumped, but answered it. If we didn't tend to this call now we would have to it as soon as the answering service sent it on.

"All Animals Hospital and Crematory, may I help you?"

"Hi, Maggie, it's Marty. It worked like a charm and Stub is on the move. We think he's headed for Walla Walla. He won't be able to get in to see Phil until tomorrow and we will be there waiting for him. I'm leaving now."

"Thanks for letting me know, Marty. I am going to be very curious what you guys learn."

"I'll call you when I know something," Marty said, and hung up.

I switched the phones over and closed up the clinic. Henry was in his carrier—he was ready to go home, too.

CHAPTER 45

The next day at home I just sort of wandered about, picking things up and setting them down. I couldn't stay focused on anything and that was bad. The ladies in the Lutheran Guild that Rose had joined were indeed thrilled with her quilt and I had several new commissions. I needed to work, but I just couldn't seem to concentrate. All I could think about was what might be going on in the prison at Walla Walla.

The day wore on. I finally decided to clean the kitchen, as that didn't take quite so much thought. Cutting out the pieces for a quilt would surely be a mistake.

It was late in the afternoon when I finished. I was contemplating a soak in the hot tub when the phone finally rang.

"It's been very interesting," Marty said. "I should be back in Spokane in a about a half an hour. Feed me tonight and I'll tell you what we learned."

"I'm already in the kitchen, Marty. You like shrimp, spinach, with a little spice to it?"

"Sounds wonderful. I'll see around five," he said, and hung up. I jumped to my feet. Now I would cook!

I put about a pound of cooked shrimp in a bowl of cold water to thaw them out. I would pull the little tail ends off then dinner would only take about 10 minutes to put together. I had just been to the store, so I actually had the green onions I needed.

Rick came in the door just as I finished de-tailing the last of the shrimp. "Marty will be here in a little while," I said. "He has some news about what happened with the decoy quilt."

"What's for dinner, that hot shrimp stuff?"*

I nodded. "I can fix that fast when Marty gets here. You want to make sure there's ice? Marty may want a drink."

Rick dug around in the freezer and I got out my oyster sauce and hot chili sauce that I get from a store called the Oriental Market. The store is on Trent just a couple of blocks west of where Trent joins with Mission Avenue. They actually have food from all over the world, China, Japan, Vietnam, Thailand, India, Korea, and Hawaii, to name just a few places. I loved to go in there and just look around and in the process I discovered several things that I wondered how I had lived without. One was hot chili sauce. This is a bright red sauce about the consistency of ketchup. More than just a drop or two on an egg would eat your face, but wow, what flavor. It was the mainstay of my hot-shrimp-on-spinach dish.

Thinking that the guys might want a bit some substance to their dinner, before I started the shrimp dish I put some Thai rice in my rice cooker and got it going. It's my favorite rice, it has a wonderful flavor and smells a bit like popcorn as it steams.

I also put a package of frozen cut leaf spinach in the microwave and started it cooking. The shrimp mixture would go onto a bed of spinach with the rice on the side. The shrimp could also go on rice or pasta without the spinach, but I really liked using the spinach.

Once the tails were off all the shrimp, I put about a tablespoon of EVOO, like the cooking show hosts call it, Extra Virgin Olive Oil, in a pan and let it get warm, but not too hot. I chopped up two green onions and let them cook for just a couple of minutes in the oil until they were soft. I did not let them brown. Then I added the shrimp. As they were cooked already, all they needed to do was get warm, but if they had been raw I would have cooked them until they turned pink and curled up. Once the shrimp were warm, I added one tablespoon of hot chili sauce and two tablespoons of oyster sauce. I turned the heat off and stirred it all together. I put the pan in the warm oven to wait.

The microwave pinged, the spinach was done. I spread it out on three plates. I like a bit of butter and salt and pepper on the spinach, too, so I added that. The shrimp mixture was spooned into its spinach bed and I added sliced hard cooked eggs around the edge. I added a scoop of rice on the side which made for very pretty plates. I covered the plates and put them back in the oven to stay warm. Rick poured me a glass of wine and we went out on the deck to get out of the warm kitchen for a few minutes while we waited for Marty.

*recipe for Spicy Shrimp Florentine at the end of the book

CHAPTER 46

▼

"That was really good, Maggie," Marty said, pushing himself away from the table. "You have to give me the recipe."

"It's bone simple," I told him. "I'll write it down for you before you leave. But, now you HAVE to tell me what went on today!"

Marty grinned. "I can see the jumping up and down that's going on in your head. Okay, here goes. But, please don't pass this around. We want to keep most of it quiet for now. I'm trusting you two, here."

"We'll be good," said Rick, holding up his hand like he was taking an oath.

"Okay," said Marty. "Well, like we guessed, Stub went straight to the state pen.

"Do you know who this Stub person is?" Rick asked. "Maggie told me she never heard of him before he called her the other day."

"I've been wondering who he is and what his connection with Phil is," I said. "Phil had certainly never mentioned knowing anybody by that name."

"We learned today at the prison that he's a guy named Dorris Eugene Stebbins," Marty said, "No surprise he wants to be called Stub. He was serving the last of his most recent sentence and was in the same cell block as Norm Seeber and Phil. One of the guards told us that those three spent so much time together the other inmates starting called them the Three Musketeers."

"And Phil roped them in with visions of big money, I suppose. I don't bet either of these guys were Mensa material, were they."

Marty laughed. "You got that right, Maggie. Plus, they were both petty thieves who had practiced their craft a few too many times and that's how they ended up at Walla Walla. Both were toying with the three strikes law and probably hoped that one last big score would set them up for life on the outside. Not that Norm needs to worry about that now, anyway."

"Okay," said Rick, "Enough about all that. What happened after Stub picked up the quilt?"

"With the locator we put in the quilt he led us right there," said Marty. "We aren't allowed to bug the visitor's area, darn it anyway, but for what went on we didn't need a bug. When Stub got there of course they had to make sure there were no weapons in the quilt. We had already alerted them that the quilt was coming and that it had a key and a locator in it."

"Key, what key?"

"I'll get to that. When Stub got to the prison they were ready. They just went over the quilt like they always would, and though they spotted the key and the locator, they left them alone. And, even though Stub as an ex-felon shouldn't have been allowed in to see Phil, they led him in to give the quilt to Phil."

"Was he thrilled to get it?"

"At first he was, and I gotta say, Maggie, that was one ugly quilt."

"Thank you, sir, it was some of my best work."

"Okay, you two," said Rick. "Then what happened?"

"Well, Phil went over that thing, held it up to the light, really looked at it. He found the dummy safety deposit box key in the binding right away."

"How and when did you do that?" I said. "You didn't tell me you were going to put a key in it, too, along with the tracking thing."

"That was sort of a last-minute inspiration the Sheriff had late last night when he was going over all of this with us. I watched the clinic this morning and after you put the quilt in the Blazer I snuck up and slipped it out for a minute and stuck the key in. For some reason that's how the Sheriff wanted to do it, so that's why I didn't come in and tell you what I was up to. Didn't want you to know, I suppose. Anyway, Phil found the key right off. He got this big grin on his face and snuck it into his pocket. If I hadn't known what he was doing I wouldn't have realized he did anything, he did it so smoothly."

"I'm so glad he's learned a skill," I snarled. "Jerk."

"Yes, a skill that served him well so far," said Marty. "But then the fun started. He examined the quilt on the back, the front, all along the binding, searching for something else, it seemed. After several minutes of this he flung the quilt on the floor and hollered, 'That rotten bitch. It was supposed to say where ...' then he stopped, realizing that everybody in the room could hear him. Stub said, 'Who, Phil? Isn't that the right quilt?'"

I started getting a sick feeling in my stomach. It didn't sound like the decoy had worked and now Stub would be coming after me again. I knew Phil would tell him to make me pay.

"Phil was still yelling," Marty said. He said, 'Yes, it's the right one. Says so right here. That fucking fat-ass told me what it looked like. She also said that she put the location of the box on the quilt but there is nothing here.' Then he got up and went back to his cell. The guards found the quilt later, torn to ribbons and stuffed into his toilet."

"Oh, man, you scared me for a minute there. I pictured Stub coming after me again."

"No, he won't be. He asked Phil if he should go find Barbara, but Phil knew she was dead. After he thinks about it he might be able to figure out where the safety deposit box is and that's probably the first place he will go when he gets out."

"But Barbara Hughes is the one who rented the box," said Rick. "How could Phil get into it?"

"I don't know the details, but Phil must also be a signer on the box. This was probably done before his attack on you in Seattle, Maggie."

"What I find puzzling is why he would want my money if he has all this stashed," I said. "That doesn't make a whole lot of sense."

"I don't know," said Marty. "Maybe he planned on Norm 'accidentally' killing you during the assault. Then, Phil could make up a tale about coming home and finding his wife dead and this man in his house. Maybe Phil would have killed Norm, too. That would have cleaned things up nicely. Phil could have claimed self-defense, then he would be free with all the money."

"Thanks a lot, Marty," said Rick. "That will help us both sleep tonight."

Marty laughed. "Sorry to give you insomnia. That's just a guess."

"So, what happens next?"

"Well, we'll be talking to Phil, for a start. If he tells us where the money is he might get an earlier parole hearing. Hopefully he will decide that once probation time is near it would be better to be free and poor than to be rich and in prison."

We talked a bit more, then Marty left, promising to let us know if anything developed. I was worn out and sleep came fast when my head hit the pillow.

CHAPTER 47

▼

The next day at the clinic we had a nearly empty afternoon schedule. That was unusual and I took the opportunity to sneak home a little early. The day before had really worn me out, although I hadn't really worked that hard. All this stuff with Phil, I suppose.

At home I picked up the phone to check for messages and heard the voice mail beep. I saw Georgia's name on the caller ID, too, good. Talking with her always brightened my day. "Call me when you get a chance," her message said.

"Hey, Geo, it's me. How are ya?"
There was a moment of silence before I heard her voice, muffled, like she was crying. "Oh, Maggie, I've been better."
"What's wrong? Did something happen?"
She sighed. "I guess so. Ron has just ..." her voice faded away, then came back.
"He's just getting more and more strange. I don't know if he's fooling around, or what's going on. But, I need to get out of here for awhile. He threatened to hit me and I'm afraid of him."
"What! Good grief, is he there?"
"No. We had an argument—he didn't get home until three o'clock this morning and when he got up this morning I asked him where he had been—I had been so worried. He got very angry and told me to butt out of his business. When I tried to explain being worried he just snarled at me, then drew back his fist like

he was going to punch me. I ran out of the room and he left, slamming the door behind him."

"Where did he go?"

"He went to work. I called and asked for him and they said he would be in a meeting for most of the day, so I know he's there for awhile anyway. Can I come sleep on your couch for a couple of days, Maggie? I hate to ask you, but I don't know what else to do. I think he needs time to cool off."

Georgia was my best friend, our friendship going back to high school days. Of course I would help her. Rick now knew about my safe "apartment" and I knew I could trust Georgia with that information, too.

"I can do better than that," I said. "Come on out. I have just the deal for you."

"Thanks so much, Mag," she said, tears trembling in her voice again. "I'll be there in a little bit."

Now I paced the floor, Henry by my side. I didn't relax until I saw Georgia's Subaru pull into the driveway. She pulled off the driveway and parked in front of the garage where my snow-plow-laden pickup sat, anticipating winter snow. I ran out to help her with her suitcase.

"I've got it," she said, swinging the first of many bags out of the trunk of her car. "You don't know how much this means to me." Tears stood in her eyes.

"You've saved me before, now it's my turn. C'mon in. Wait until you see what I have for you."

Like Rick, Georgia's eyes about popped out of her head when I showed her the secret staircases and the underground apartment. She was fascinated by the story of Eleanor and Larry Branson, too. I showed her how to go outside through the door that led into the utility room in the small daylight basement. From there she could get outside and she could come and go without having to come up into the upstairs house at all. I helped her hang up her and clothes and then said, "Let's go up and have some coffee. You look like you could use some." She nodded and we went up the hidden staircase and into the living room.

"I can hardly believe what this house is really like," she said. "Why did the builders put that basement part in?"

"Larry Branson had it done when they built the house. He wanted to have a safe haven for his family should they need it. Rather like the fallout shelters people were building in the 1950s and 60s during the Cold War. My dad wanted for us to have one, but when my mom found out that there would be a hump in the yard with a stove pipe sticking out, she put her foot down. She would rather die of radiation poisoning than have 'people' commenting on her odd-looking yard. Not that there would have been a lot to come up for after an atom bomb attack anyway."

Georgia smiled, good. I was hoping to lighten her mood. "Yeah, my folks talked about doing that too. Somehow, though, they just never got to it. This underground apartment is how all the houses should be built in tornado country, that's for sure."

"I agree with you. I can't imagine having to worry about having my house blow away every tornado season. You can stay as long as you like. I'll give you a spare key to the house and show you where the hidden button is in the utility room that opens the door to the basement living part for when you want to come back in. I'll need to show you how to disarm the security system if we're not here, too. I don't think I told you about the studio getting broken into or Norm's visit, did I?"

Again her eyes were wide. When I got to the part about shooting at Norm's feet she jumped up.

"You SHOT at him? Maggie, I don't believe it! Wait, yes I do. Aren't you afraid he'll come back?"

"Not a chance. Luckily for me, he's dead."

"You didn't …"

Her expression made me laugh. "No, I didn't actually kill him. He kidnapped Sully and Rick and I found her. Norm came back to where he was keeping her just as I left. He started to chase me, then the cops started chasing him. He crashed into a power pole and killed himself."

"And you were going to tell me about this when?" Georgia frowned at me.

"I did call you a couple of times and left messages with Ron. You never called me back."

Georgia sighed. "Well, now it's my turn to tell a story."

CHAPTER 48

She sat back down on the sofa and picked up her coffee. She took a small sip then set her cup on the table. "Remember all the conversations we used to have about abused women? How we couldn't understand how a woman would 'let' herself be pushed around like that?"

"Geo, Ron didn't ..."

She held up her hand to silence me. "No, like I told you on the phone he never hit me, but I don't know how long that would have lasted. It's funny how it works." She plopped back against the sofa cushions. "First it was little things, like being picky about foods he has always liked, the laundry not being just so, stuff that was easy to fix. But, the more I fixed, the more he found wrong. Then, he started opening my mail. My mom sent me a check for my birthday, but I never got it. She called after a couple of months when it hadn't shown on her bank statement. She said at first she was a little peeved, thinking I wasn't going to thank her, but then when the check wasn't cashed, she called."

"Did you ask Ron about it?"

"Yes, right away. He denied it every coming. This sounded okay, things occasionally do get lost in the mail. But, then I didn't get a bank statement for a couple of months, either. I was able to get a copy from the bank, so that wasn't a problem. Again, Ron said that nothing had come for me."

"How was he able to intercept your mail? Aren't you mostly home during the day?"

"Yeah, but he said he really liked opening the mailbox and finding things in it. He told me he had always liked doing that, even when he was little. I found that somewhat endearing and left the mail for him to pick up when he came home.

But, after my mom sent me a replacement check and I didn't get that one either, well ..."

"I assume you stopped leaving the mail for him, then."

"Well, sort of. I started watching for the mailman and after he came I would go check the box. I would leave any junk mail that was addressed to me, along with any mail of Ron's. Anything else I took out. He figured that out last week, though. He put a lock on the box and he had the only key."

"Has he lost his mind, Georgia? He was never like this before."

Georgia shook her head. "Not to this extent, no. He has always been a bit jealous of any of my friends or any time I spent away from him, but that seemed normal enough. He never forbid me to go out or visit anybody, until last night—or I should say this morning, that is."

"What did he do?"

"Well, I told you about the argument and him leaving. What I didn't realize until I went out to the key rack is that he took my car keys with him, too. He didn't know I kept a spare set in my purse. Thank goodness he didn't take that, too."

"But that wouldn't stop you. You could just call a cab or something."

She smiled, but in was a smile of bitterness, not amusement. "Oh, there's more. When I went to leave I discovered that he bolted the doors shut from the outside. I was a virtual prisoner. I can't image why he didn't think to cut the phone lines, too. I did get several hang up calls today that I assumed were wrong numbers or somebody fooling around but know I think it was probably him calling to make sure I was home."

"So what did you do, go out a window?"

"No, it was even easier than that. I suppose he forgot about the outside cellar door that leads into the basement that we hardly ever use. That door is locked from the inside with just a simple latch. It's all that's needed as the basement door is also locked from the inside, too. It was easy to open both doors and just walk out. I packed up as much stuff as I could in all of our suitcases. I'm never going back, Maggie."

"I guess not. But, what is going to happen when he comes home and you are gone?"

Tears started down Georgia's face. "That scares me, Maggie, and now I'm afraid I'll put you in danger, too."

"Hey, best friend, I've there before." For a minute I remembered what it had been like, hiding under an overturned boat near the docks in Ilwaco, praying that a killer wouldn't find me. I shivered.

"I'll leave," Georgia said, getting up. "I don't want to risk you getting hurt."

"No, you won't," I said, pushing her back to her seat. "This calls for a fresh pot of coffee and some butterscotch cookies." I handed her the cookie jar. "Here, start on these. Then we'll figure something out."

I knew the first thing we needed to do was hide Georgia's car. I figured it would fit in the back of the garage where the pickup slumbered, waiting for winter. There was a back door in the garage, too. The driveway was very primitive back there, but Georgia would be able to get in and out without having to move the truck every time. The Subaru would be somewhat hidden, but Ron still might be able to see it. Hmmmm. While Georgia crunched on cookies and I filled the coffee pot, I pondered.

CHAPTER 49

▼

"I know what to do!" I said, snapping my fingers and making Georgia jump.

"About what?"

"I was thinking about how we could hide your car but still have it easily accessible for you. You can park your car behind the truck in the garage and I figured out how to hide it from Ron. If he comes here looking for you, that is."

"Oh, I bet he will. He's going to be furious that I got away and I'm his possession, after all, or so he thinks."

"Yeah, he probably will come here looking for you. I was trying to think of a way to hide your car so it couldn't be seen behind the truck when I remembered something. Back when I was married to Phil we rented a house in Seattle while we looked for one to buy. Only half of the basement was finished, the rest was accessible as crawl space only. One day when I was outside I noticed a couple of windows that I had never seen from the inside. I couldn't stand it; I had to know where these windows were. I went into the crawl space, you could actually walk in there if you walked bent over. The walls where I saw the windows from the outside were blank, no windows there."

"How was that possible?"

I giggled. "That's where my idea for hiding your car came from. For some reason, the owner of the house had stapled a piece of dark brown burlap to the floor joist above that hung down to the dirt floor. Until you got right up next to and touched it, it just looked like a wall. When I lifted the burlap I could see the windows."

"So how can that work to hide my car?"

"Well, I'll rat around and find some dark fabric. We can hang it up behind the pickup and unless Ron goes into the garage and really looks, your car should be invisible."

"Good idea, Maggie! Need any help?"

"Sure. I have some fabric in mind, in fact. I picked up a big piece of what I though was cotton at Goodwill one day. It turned out to be a polyester cotton blend that put out a very strange odor when I ironed it. I won't ever use it in a quilt, but you know me and my eleventh commandment: Thou Shalt Throw Nothing Away. I still have it around here somewhere. The staple gun is in the drawer out by the washer. You grab that and I go look for that material."

It only took a bit of searching and I found the fabric. It was a huge chunk of material, but even so we had just enough pieces to make a curtain across the back of the garage. We went out to the end of the driveway and studied our workmanship. The pickup looked like it was parked right up against the back wall of the garage. As long as Ron didn't actually go into the garage and look closer, Georgia's Subaru was invisible. We shared a high five and went back to the house.

CHAPTER 50

▼

When Rick got home Georgia was in the lower part of the house unpacking. She had about filled her car with suitcases and it took us several trips to get it all in. Rick hadn't spotted her car and that was reassuring. Our makeshift wall must be working.

"I heard from Marty today," Rick said. "He said that Phil is indeed ready to deal with them; that he's real sick of being in prison."

My stomach turned over. "So, he's getting out?"

Rick shook his head. "Not for good, no. He still has to do a few more years, but his chance for parole will come up sooner if he is able to find the money and give it back."

"But, how can he do that? He doesn't know where the safety deposit box is."

"Not yet. There was something he hadn't talked about until today. There is a safe deposit box at a bank that he and Barbara Hughes shared. She used to pay the rent a year in advance and he thinks that she may have left him the answer or the money there. But, he won't tell anybody which bank or the box number. That was part of his deal, that he gets to go to the box himself. Next week somebody from the sheriff's office will go pick him up and take him to the box. Then, hopefully for him, anyway, to the money."

"That's pretty scary; him being out."

"Marty said it will be okay, that Phil will be in handcuffs the whole time."

"Still. Brrrrrrr. Gives me the shivers."

"It'll be okay. What was that?" Rick straightened up and looked down at the floor. "It sounds like somebody is downstairs."

"There is. Georgia is going to stay with us for a few days. Ron has gone nuts, tried to lock her in the house. She was able to get out, though. I told her she would be safe here until she can get some things taken care of. I hope you don't mind."

"Heavens, no. I'm glad we have a safe house for her. What happened, anyway?"

I spent a few minutes telling Rick the story Georgia had told me earlier.

"Wow," he said, "What a mess. What is she going to do?"

"I think in the morning she plans to call a lawyer. Ron's distrust of her will be to her benefit, in a way. She has her own checking account, credit cards, and the Subaru is registered to her. She at least will have some money to file for divorce. I also suggested she find out about a restraining order, too."

"That sounds like a good idea. Boy, I'm glad there's nothing exciting going on in our lives right now!" Rick went to change out of his work clothes and I turned back to dinner preparations.

I awoke with a start. What had I heard? The room was silent but for Rick's soft breathing. There wasn't even any wind tonight. But, something had ... there is was again, a low growl.

I slipped out of bed, grabbing my big silver Maglite from the nightstand. It would make a good club if I needed one. The noise was coming from the living room.

As quietly as I could I walked down the short hall from the bedroom. The growling that woke me up was still going on, low and vicious.

I could see into the living room from the trace of moonlight coming in through the windows. There did not appear to be anybody there, but there was a black lump on the floor. I turned my flashlight on and aimed the beam in that direction. The growling intensified into a scream of rage and I stepped back, scared of the beast that hunched in the middle of the floor.

CHAPTER 51

▼

"Oh, my God, Henry, you scared me to death."

Henry was crouched over Barbara's funny lumpy quilt in the middle of the floor, the hair on his back standing straight up. His ears were laid back, his eyes gleamed a cat-from-hell red, and his mouth was open in a savage snarl. His paws were clenched into fists, claws dug deep in the quilt. There must be a mouse or something trapped in it. I had never seen him act like this. I took a step back. This sweet house cat looked like a wild animal and I was a little afraid of him.

Suddenly, his fur smoothed out. He pulled his claws away from the quilt and started toward me, pearling and meowing in his "kill" voice. The wild panther was transformed back into a happy house cat. He wound around my legs and I could hear him purring.

With some hesitation, I picked him up. As usual, he clamped his front paws around my neck and began to purr and snort into my ear.

"What's with you?" I asked him. "You catch a mouse?"

All he did was squint his eyes happily and me and work his paws on my shoulders. I took him over to my chair.

"Here, you stay put for a minute while I go check out your victim."

I set Henry down and he watched me intently as I went over to the quilt. Gingerly I reached out and took hold of the very corner with my thumb and first finger. I was prepared for a mouse to dash out from underneath or to find a mouse corpse. But, nothing prepared me for what I did find.

CHAPTER 52

▼

What I found was … nothing. There was no mouse, or bug, or anything else that looked like prey. I gave the quilt a shake, but nothing fell off of it. Henry had been having an attack of rage at the quilt itself. I looked over at my chair. Henry was watching me, but he didn't seem any more interested than if I were shaking out a new piece of fabric. I wondered what would happen if I got the quilt near him. Not being sure how he would react, I tossed it over the arm of the chair. He started to rub his face against the French knots that covered the quilt. His paws continued to knead the chair cushion and his purring had not stopped.

I stood and watched him for a few minutes, but nothing changed. I shook my head, puzzled. What could have made him so angry that he was attacking the quilt like that? Maybe there was a mouse that darted away unseen—that was probably the answer. Henry certainly looked fine now. He was curled up against the arm of the chair where the quilt had landed and he was fast asleep. My feet were cold and it was way too early to be up and about. I went back to bed.

Over breakfast I told Rick, who had slept through the whole thing, the story of Henry and the quilt.

"Why would a cat act like that?" I asked.

"Who knows," Rick said. "They can be such odd animals. I would bet on a mouse, though. It probably got away but he thought it was still under the quilt. That may be why he attacked it like he did."

"Boy, it was really something. I wish you could have seen Henry and the way he was acting. I was actually afraid of him."

"It's a good thing you didn't try to approach him or touch him until he calmed down," Rick said. "He might have really lit into you."

"Yeah, I know. I get chills just talking about it. He looked like a black panther crouching over a dead wildebeest."

"I'm off," said Rick, standing up. "Work calls. See you later." He bent down for a kiss then was out the door. I put the dishes in the dishwasher and went to the quilting studio. I had a couple of customers' quilts to finish.

I bent over a lovely double wedding ring quilt my friend Mary Planter had made. I was going to quilt a heart motif in the middle of each ring, but I had to draw the design on before I tried to sew it. I had enough trouble sewing along drawn lines, but I would be hopeless if I tried to do this design freehand. My water soluble pen had just touched the fabric in the first ring when a loud pounding on the studio door almost startled me out of my shoes.

In the past I would probably have just innocently opened the door, but recent events had made me a bit cautious.

"Who is it?"

"It's Ron Delman and I am here for my wife," an angry male voice shouted. "Open the door, dammit!"

"No, Ron, I won't. Georgia is not here, anyway."

"Then where the hell is she? I know she called you yesterday." Ron thumped on the door again. I could hear Brandy barking in the yard, but there was a fence between her and Ron.

"Georgia just called and told me she had to cancel our lunch date," I said. "We didn't really talk."

"That's a bunch of crap. I know she's here and I'm not leaving until you produce her. Got that?"

"Yes, Ron, but I tell you she's not here." I wasn't even lying. Georgia had gone to see about a lawyer and a restraining order against Ron. I hoped she would gone a long time.

Ron beat another thunderous tattoo on the door. I was glad it was a metal door, but I also knew that if he were determined, he would get in. I walked over to the little table by the potbellied stove and picked up the phone. This getting threatened by angry men was getting to be a routine for me.

Within minutes a sheriff's deputy was pulling into the yard. Almost before Ron could react he found himself sitting in the back of the deputy's car in handcuffs. This time when there was a knock on the door I didn't mind opening it.

The deputy look down the details and drove away with Ron fuming in the back seat. I knew he would be out of jail quickly, but I hoped he wouldn't try that trick again.

CHAPTER 53

▼

I told Georgia to plan on staying in the downstairs house as long as she needed to. Ron made a couple of more trips out to try and find her, but after being taken away by the sheriff both times, he gave up. They told him one more time and there would be worse charges other than trespassing and disturbing the peace. Georgia had a restraining order against Ron and I also got one forbidding him from contacting me at home or at work; I had gotten a couple of profanity-filled irate calls from Ron at the clinic, too.

Georgia had a lawyer and the divorce was in process. She discovered that Ron not only had become outrageously controlling, he had also been hiding assets and possessions from her for years. His defense was that she was not smart enough to be trusted knowing how much money they had; that she would have taken it and spent it. Georgia alternated between being devastated by hurt and furious with the insults.

But for all that, she was a very courteous house guest. Rick and I hardly even knew she was living under our feet. Plus, I was glad to find out from her that little noise from above made it down to her ears.

"I can't thank you enough for letting me stay here, Maggie," she said as we drank coffee on the deck. "Until the legalities are done I couldn't have afforded to rent a place; not that I don't intend on paying you for the time I spend here."

"Good grief, Geo, don't even think about it," I said. "I haven't noticed any real change in any of the bills, so you must not be using much electricity or water. You let me stay with you all that time after I came back from Seattle, after all. This is just payback."

"Well, okay, if you're sure. Although this place is a lot nicer than my little granny flat."

"That granny flat was perfect for me and the cats," I said. "Hopefully you will be able to find a place of your own you like as much as the one I found."

"I'm sure I'll be able to find a place I like," she said, "But there is no other place like this, I'm sure."

You are so right, I thought. This is the most unique house I had ever seen and I felt honored to own it. I hoped I was doing Eleanor and Larry Branson, the couple who built it, right by their house.

"How's the house hunt going, anyway? Brian being helpful?" Brian was my Realtor for this house. I felt I owed him a commission after all the fruitless time he had spent trying to find Rose a place.

"Brian's great. I really like him. I have a couple of houses that I'm looking at. My favorite is a little art and crafts-style bungalow in Millwood. I have never lived out in the valley, but that has always been one of my favorite areas. It would be good not to have to drive so far to work, now that I am working for Dr. Bryant out on Evergreen Road."

"How are you liking that?"

"It's fine. He's really a nice guy and reception work is reception work, after all. He has somebody else who works at his north side office, and it's nice that I don't have to travel back and forth like he and his medical assistant do. The only problem I'm having is that there is so much to learn about the various insurances and what is paid and what isn't, both for routine foot care and surgeries. You're lucky you don't have to deal with all that at the animal clinic."

"Do I ever know it. A few people have that pet insurance, but it's pretty straightforward as to what is covered and what isn't. Plus, it's only one business and one office, too."

Georgia laughed, something I was glad to see. She had been so somber lately. "That would really make it nice, to not have both a regular foot care clinic and a surgery center to think about. Other than that, it's a good office to work in. I had no idea podiatry could be so involved. I used to think all podiatrists did was trim toenails and grind off calluses. But, there's so much more to it. I never knew that a callus can form if there is a bump of bone putting pressure on the skin above it, or that corns were just calluses on steroids, so to speak. Really interesting. The only bad thing is there is this Dr. Sidek that is subleasing the office space when Dr. Bryant is seeing patients at the north office. I am at the valley office four days a week, though, and so I get to see this Sidek character in action. He is a rude, arrogant man and I don't think he's a very good surgeon, from what I've overheard from his patients when they come in complaining. The one thing that keeps me sane, though, is that I don't work for him. He has his own receptionist and medical assistant. Plus, Ron will never think to look for me in a foot clinic. I wouldn't be surprised if he has called all the dentists in town looking for me, though. That's one reason I'll stay out of dental offices as an employee for awhile."

Maggie and I traded patient stories for awhile. Mine were a bit more varied, coming from the ICU at the hospital in Seattle where I had worked, but hers were interesting too.

"Well," Georgia said, "I better get myself pulled together. Brian is coming to pick me up. We're going to go and talk to the people who are selling the house in Millwood. It's actually part of an estate and has sat empty for several months. I am hoping they will be willing to hold it for me until the divorce is final and I have some money."

"Do you think there's a chance they will do that?"

"I think so. The house hasn't had any updating or fresh paint or anything done to it for a long time, in fact, the kitchen and bathroom look vintage 1930, the year the house was built. Brian said that they haven't gotten any offers for anything near their asking price, and I offered just a bit less. He said they aren't in a big rush to sell and they are willing to accept my price. Now if they will just be willing to wait for the money."

"You won't mind fixing it up?" I asked.

"No, not a bit. That way I can have what I want. I can't wait to have a dog or a cat, or maybe both, again." Georgia stood up. "So, what's your plan for the rest of today?"

"I guess I'll just do a bit of housework and then finish up those quilts I was working on. I hope Rick doesn't have to spend his whole Saturday at the Cox place tending to that sick mule."

CHAPTER 54

▼

It was dinner time by the time Rick got home. The mule had turned into a real challenge, after all. He entertained me with stories about the Cox's border collie trying to herd the rest of the mules around in the pasture. These were big mules, much larger than any sheep, but that hadn't stopped the dog from trying.

My quilts were done, too. It was nice not to have any projects hanging over me, but I knew that wouldn't last. It was just the way it went; I either had too much to do or not enough.

The next morning I sat and watched Henry rub his face over Barbara's quilt again. His anger from a few nights ago was gone. I would probably never know what set him off. I watched while he rubbed his face then curled up on the quilt for a nap. I hadn't heard from Marty and I was very curious about what had gone on at the prison.

I spent the day just generally pulling things back together in the studio. When I am hot on a project I tend to just pile up the fabrics I am using on the floor next to my cutting table and sewing machines. Ditto for any new fabric I get during this time. I sorted everything out by color and then put each color in its proper bin. That made it so much easier; when I needed a green fabric I could just pull out the green bin. For the first time in weeks I could see the floor.

I heard the phone ringing as I went through the secret door into the kitchen.

"Maggie, it's Marty."

"Hi, Marty. I've been wanting to hear from you ..."

"I'm in a real rush, Maggie," he said, cutting me off. "Listen, I needed to call and warn you."

I felt a chill. "Warn me about what?"

Marty sighed, sounding disgusted. "Somebody really dropped the ball. Phil Scott escaped today."

"What!" My knees buckled and I dropped into a chair. "How did that happen?"

"I don't know all the details, but it went something like this: After Stub took him that quilt you made, Phil called his lawyer. He told the lawyer that he would lead the cops to the money, if his sentence would be reduced. The lawyer told him he would work on that, but taking the cops to the money would certainly be in Phil's favor. Some yahoo, probably thinking he was a real hot shot, arranged to take Phil out on a day pass. While they were traveling to where Phil said the bank was, Phil managed to get away."

"But, didn't they have him handcuffed, or something?" I asked.

"I don't know. Maybe not. He is a model prisoner, they said."

"Well, that's just great. He has to know that isn't the real quilt, if he knew how Barbara made it to tell him where the money is. Now I suppose he'll come after me."

"That's just what I'm afraid of, Maggie. Is there someplace safe you can go?"

I sat and thought for a minute. There was another bedroom downstairs. I could move in with Georgia until Phil was caught. "Yes. There's actually a safe house built in the basement of my place. It's invisible from the outside and you are only the third person to know about it. I'll show it to you next time you're here."

"If you think that will be safe, okay. In the meantime, I'll have a car at your house when you are home. I'll also have your guard drop off a GPS locator. Put it in your purse and don't go anywhere without it, okay?"

"Marty, you are scaring me. Do you really think all this is necessary?"

"Yes, I do, Maggie. Phil got a hold of the deputy's gun and shot him during the escape. Luckily, the deputy was wearing a Kevlar vest. He got the wind knocked out of him and will have a pretty good bruise, but he's okay."

"... and the gun is where?"

"Phil has the gun, Maggie. That's why we're so concerned. There should already be a car at your house. Stay alert, Maggie. Try not to go anywhere alone. The deputy will follow you to work and then when you are ready I'll give you a number to call for an escort home."

"Oh, Marty, this is going to be awful. I hate being scared like this."

"I know, Maggie, and I'm sorry. Hopefully we'll pick Phil up really quickly."

"I hope so, too. Thanks, Marty. Keep me posted what's going on, okay?"

I hung up the phone and heard a knock at the door. My heart pounding, I went into the living room.

I could see the deputy sheriff standing on the porch, but I still didn't unfasten the screen door and let him in until I knew for sure it wasn't Phil in disguise.

"Martin Adams sent me," he said. "He told me to give you this." The deputy handed me a small black box with various dials and knobs on the front. "This is a GPS locator. Push this button and turn it on every morning, or if you have to go anyplace at night, even if you are with somebody. That's all you have to do. It starts transmitting a signal immediately." He handed me an AC converter. "See this hole on the bottom? Plug in this charger overnight, every night. That will keep the GPS battery charged. My name is Ken, by the way, and I'll be your primary guard."

I hadn't been able to get a word in until now. "Good to meet you, Ken. Please feel free to come to the house if you need anything, like a bathroom."

He grinned. "Thanks, that will save me trips into the bushes. Now, I need you to tell me what your schedule is."

After the deputy went back to his car, I went around and checked every window in the house to make sure they were either locked, or that the locks that prevented them from opening more than about two inches were in place. Larry Branson had McVay Brothers Siding and Windows put in that type when the house was built. There were neat little tabs that flicked out to prevent the window from opening too far. They could be retracted, though, to open the window up all the way to allow for emergency escape. I made sure all the tabs were in the locking position.

I also made sure my pistol was loaded and in the drawer of the little table by the front door, where I could get to it quickly.

Next I called Sonitrol to let them know what was going on. I wanted them to respond quickly if there was an alarm.

"You have made sure all your doors and windows are secure, correct?" The Sonitrol representative asked.

"Yes. My only concern is my dog door. It might be large enough for someone to get through. What can I do about that? I need for my dog to be able to get in and out."

"We have a device that will work well for you," the Sonitrol man said. "It's an electric switch that goes on the door. You put a small box on your dog's collar and turn it on. The door will open when the dog gets close enough, but otherwise it is locked. You can set a timer and it and it will automatically close when the time is up. Just watch your dog go in and out a few times and see how long it takes. Most dogs got through their dog doors really fast, in a matter of seconds. If anybody tries to force the door, or to hold it open for too long, an alarm will sound here, just like your other door and window alarms."

"That sounds great. How much?" I asked. I didn't really care about the cost. Assuming it wasn't a ridiculous amount, I was going to have the alarm installed.

He promised to come out later in the day to install the dog door alarm. Once Sonitrol had come and gone I felt much safer. I hated this, though. It was like I was in jail, instead of Phil, who belonged there.

CHAPTER 55

▼

Ken was relieved by Brandon, who spent the night near my house. Rick was not thrilled with to have cops at the door, but he was also glad they were there to protect us.

"I hope they catch that Phil character pretty soon," he said as we were headed for bed. "I'll sleep better when I know he's back in prison."

"You and me both," I said. "I hate this."

The next morning Brandon followed me to work. He handed me a card as he walked me to the clinic door. "Call this number when you are ready to leave for home or if you go anywhere during the day. We don't want you out and about without at least minimum protection."

"Thanks, Brandon. I'll see you tomorrow, I guess."

With a wave, the deputy drove off. I went into the clinic and sat down at my desk. Hopefully Phil wouldn't be so stupid as to try something here.

Meanwhile, I would look at that quilt again. I had stuffed it into a bag and brought it along, hoping for time to really study it. I pulled it out of the bag and spread it out on my desk. There has to something Rick and I were missing, there had to be. We had looked at it from all angles, yet could not see anything special or that looked like any sort of instructions.

I only got a few minutes to ponder the quilt. The phone rang and the day was busy from that point on, lots of animals coming and going. It was late in the afternoon when the inspiration hit me. We had a fluoroscope machine in the back. This showed live action x-rays and was very handy to assess joint function, for one thing. Jeanne came out to put a file away.

"Hey, Jeanne, what to help me with something?"

"Sure," she said, "What's up?"

"Well, you know about his quilt that supposedly contains directions to some hidden money? Rick and I have looked at it every way except inside out, and that will be next!, but we haven't been able to find anything. You want to help me run it through the C-arm?"

The fluoroscope was essentially a TV monitor mounted on a stand. Extended out from the stand was a long, adjustable arm with a C-shaped piece mounted on the end. The part that needed fluoroscopic examination was placed in the open part of the C. I suppose that's why it was called a C-arm.

It took a bit of flopping the quilt around, but Jeanne and I finally managed to scan the whole thing. I got a good look at the bones in both of our hands, but we found nothing in the quilt.

"Rats," I said. "I was hoping maybe she used radio-opaque thread, or something. Well, I guess the next step would be to take it apart. What a chore that will be, though, I'll have to cut off all those French knots. Thanks, Jeanne, I better get back to the front."

I tossed the quilt over the front counter and was pondering how I was going to take it apart when Aileen, our mail carrier, came in with the day's delivery. She stroked Henry, who was up rubbing his face on the quilt again.

"That's certainly an interesting thing," she said. "Where did you get it?"

"Oh, Aileen, that is such a long story. Some time you and I will have to get together on your day off and I'll tell you. The short version is that is supposed to be a treasure map, so to speak, telling where some stolen money was hidden."

"Really? What are the clues?"

"That's just it," I said. "I'm so frustrated by the fact that I can't find anything that looks like any sort of directions on it."

"There's no marks on it of any kind?"

"No, nothing that we can find, anyway. I was just thinking about how much work it will be to take it apart; the inside is the only place we haven't looked."

She ran her fingers over the French knots. "Why would anybody put all these knots on here. They don't spell anything, do they?"

"Not that I can figure out. They seem so random, in rows, but spaced out so funny. Then there are big gaps, too. I don't know."

Alice continued to run her fingers over the knots then suddenly stopped, pulling her fingers away as if the quilt were hot.

"What's the matter? Did something poke you?"

"No," she said, "Not that. I just had a mental flash. My sister was blind. When she was little she learned to read Braille and I learned a little bit, too. It's been a long time, but I think I found a couple of words here that I remembered. I bet you these knots are tied to mimic Braille. That could be the answer to your puzzle; you've been looking right at it."

I felt my mouth drop open. "Of course, how obvious. Is that what you've been trying to tell me, Henry, with all that face rubbing?" Henry was sitting and looking at me with a yellow-eyed squint. He was probably thinking I was hopelessly stupid.

"Can you read it, Aileen?"

"No, it's been too many years and I never was really literate in Braille. But, you could call the Lilac Blind Foundation. I bet they would either be able to read it for you right there or find somebody who could." She glanced at her watch. "I better get out of here and finish my route. I'm going to want to know the end of this one," she said.

I sat and ran my fingers over the knots. How amazing. I grabbed the phone book to look up the Lilac Blind Foundation. Before I picked up the phone I looked at the quilt again. It seemed to almost glow with a supernatural light. Now I really knew how valuable it was and why Phil wanted it so badly. I decided to put it someplace safe before I did another thing.

When Rick and I were trying to figure out if Lynda Mancusco was smuggling drugs through the clinic, we kept all kinds of notes and information in the office. We didn't want to risk taking the file home, but we worried about it being discovered in the clinic, too. We ended up stashing it on a ceiling tile in the dropped ceiling. This still sounded like a good hiding spot. I pulled out the little stepstool we used to change the lights in the ceiling and lifted a tile away from the suspension frame. I set the quilt on another tile. Good, it wasn't heavy enough to make the tile sag. I replaced the tile I removed and dusted off my hands. There. The quilt was safe from all but the most determined search.

CHAPTER 56

▼

For the next few days nothing happened. Marty said there was no sign of Phil anywhere. The police and sheriff's department had no idea where he might be. I wondered if he had recovered the money by himself and was happily lying in the sun in some warm place. I was starting to feel safe again.

My own bit of the world was starting to feel normal again, too. Rick's mother had found several lady friends to lunch with, she even joined Stroh's and did the water aerobics class three days a week. Georgia was pleased that the people who owned the house that she wanted would be willing to wait for their money until the divorce was final. Ron had not shown up at my house since his last trip away in a prowl car and his calls to the clinic had stopped. The fabric wall Georgia and I put up had worked, too; Ron had not spotted her car behind it. We hoped he had become convinced that she wasn't here.

Rick seemed to have regained his equilibrium following his father's death and we started talking about specific wedding dates. I almost didn't notice my police guardians anymore either; they had become part of my landscape.

I was a little early to work Friday morning, but, as usual, Jeanne had beaten me there. I could see the back end of her Toyota Tundra peeking out from behind the building. I don't know how she did it. I waved good-bye to my deputy escort and headed toward the clinic. I will actually enjoy being inside today, I thought, looking at the gray, rainy sky.

"Morning, Jeanne," I called out as I opened the front door. She didn't answer, but that was not unusual. If she were in the farthest back corner of the building, or if there was a dog barking, she wouldn't be able to hear me. I hung my coat up and went to my desk.

"Don't get too cozy, there, Maggie. We got work to do."

I'm not normally a screamer, but the sight of Phil coming out of Rick's office got me going. "Good God, what are you doing here? How did you get in?"

Phil smiled, a smile I did not like. "I just followed your cute little doc in and locked her up in the back, easy as pie," he said. "She won't be bothering us."

"Did you hurt her, you bastard, you better not have. Now, you get the hell out of here; I'm calling the cops." I lunged toward the phone.

Phil leaped across the floor and grabbed my arm, twisting it up behind my back. I grit my teeth; I would not let him know he was hurting me.

"Not so fast, bitch. You and I got things to do. Get going."

He started to drag me toward the door. "Let me have my coat, jerk. It's cold outside."

"Sure, go ahead. You might not need it for long, though." Phil pulled my coat off the hook and threw it at me. He shoved me toward the door. "My car's out in the back, get moving."

As soon as we were out the door I opened my mouth to yell. The sudden stab in my side made me gasp instead.

"Make a sound and you're dead right now," he said. "I don't really want to kill you right now, but I don't care if I do, either. First, you are going to give me what I want."

Phil shoved me into the back seat of a beat up old sedan. He had prepared for this, there was a metal grate between the front and back seats and there were no door handles or window winding cranks in the back. Once inside, I could not get out. He had tinted the windows such a dark color that I could scarcely see out, either. Nobody would be able to see in, I was sure.

"Now we are going to your house," he said. "You will go in and get me my quilt and then, if you're lucky, I'll let you go. I already shot a cop, I got nothing to lose."

I ground my teeth. Where was that .38, now that I really needed it? "It's not there," I said. "I gave it to the sheriff."

"Well, then, we'll just have to get it back, won't we. I shouldna known you'd do something like that, little Miss Goody Two-Shoes. That's okay, I planned for that too. I'll just have to stash you away until that boyfriend of yours can get me my property." Phil pulled the car to the side of the road. "In the meantime, you don't need to know where we are going." Phil pulled out a piece of black plastic. He hung it on the metal grate that separated the front from the back seats then pulled back out onto Trent. Once that plastic was in place, I was riding in a cave. I could see nothing. I reached in my coat pocket. Yes! My keys were still there. I pulled them out and using the little disc that was actually a screwdriver, started to scratch at the glass. If I could just get a bit of the tinting off I would be able to see out.

"Don't waste your time," Phil snarled. "I also figured you'd try screwing around with the windows, sneaky bitch that you are. I put the tint on the outside." He laughed. "It won't last as long, but by the time it falls off I won't care."

Defeated, I slumped back on the seat. My purse was on the floor in the clinic where I had dropped it, its GPS unit merrily signaling away. Marty and the others would have no problem finding the purse, finding me would be a bit tougher. I needed to try and figure out where we were going.

I knew we had turned right as we left the clinic and we hadn't made any turns since. We were heading west, but I had no idea how far we had gone. It was like riding in the fog; time and distance seemed altered. I felt the car slow, this could be the light at Evergreen, or Pines. I didn't think we had gone as far as Argonne Road, but I couldn't be sure.

I heard the turn indicator come on. Phil stopped momentarily and then turned left. But, where? I had no idea.

CHAPTER 57

▼

I felt the car moving slowly down a slight bumpy, downhill, track. It was paved, but not smooth pavement, like one of the main streets would have been. I didn't feel us bump over any railroad tracks, and all the roads leading off Trent except for Argonne, where the road made the plunge under the tracks, had Burlington Northern crossings. Had Phil pulled into a driveway?

He stopped the car and reached in to pull me out. Before I had a chance to look around at all, I felt a bag go over my head. Then, holding one of my arms painfully bent behind my back, he marched me over uneven ground where I could feel tall, wet, grass brushing against my legs.

I heard a door open. Phil shoved me inside and I fell to my hands and knees on a splintery wood floor. I heard the door slam and a lock engage. Wherever I was, I was locked in.

I pulled the bag off my head and looked around. I was in what looked like a abandoned stable. In addition to a tiny open area, there were two stalls and some random bits of tack that told me this stable was used for horses at one time. The only light came from windows high on the walls that were covered with a frosty coating. Light came in, but I could not see out.

"As soon as you leave, asshole, I'm punching one of those windows out," I muttered to the empty stable. "You think you can keep me here, you got another think coming."

The door opened and Phil walked in. He hadn't heard me, but he had plans, anyway. I could see that. He grabbed my arm and pushed me down onto the floor. I felt a handcuff snick closed around my wrist.

"Give me your other arm," he said.

"Go fuck yourself," was my intelligent and original response.

I felt his knee go into my back. "Give me your arm or I break your neck," he said.

I fought as hard as I could, but found myself getting increasingly short of breath as the pressure on my back increased. Finally I gave up. He grabbed my other arm and closed the handcuff around it, too. He made sure they were tight. There would be no hope of working my hands out of them. Phil yanked me to my feet. There was a cot on one side of the stable; he threw me on it. I felt his hands all over my chest and belly. Then, he ran his hand into my pants. I spit in his face.

I heard the slap before I felt it. My ears rang and I saw stars. "You aren't worth even raping, you piece of shit, at least not right now. Maybe you'll be friendlier in a day or two."

Phil stomped to the door and let himself out. I heard the lock click shut on the other side.

"I'm going to go call on your boyfriend," he yelled. I heard the car engine start up and then all was still.

I collapsed back on the cot, letting the tears I'd been holding back flow. If I had thought the time in Seattle was bad, boy, was I wrong. This seemed hopeless. My little screwdriver saved the day when I was trapped in a building once before, but it wouldn't unlock handcuffs, that I knew.

My nose was running and I couldn't even wipe it. I turned my face over and rubbed it against the coarse blanket on the cot. There, that helped.

"Stop your bawling and figure this out, Maggie," I said. Somehow saying the words out loud helped. I took another look around. Phil was smart, but not real smart. He had secured this building, but he hadn't looked around on the inside, that was obvious. Now that I did, I saw lots of things that might help me.

Whoever kept horses here had done their own shoeing. There were several tools scattered around, pliers to pulls nails from the hoof, files, picks, and most importantly, the odd shaped handles that I saw sticking out of a pile of burlap bags. They looked like the tool that actually was used to clip the edges of the hooves. I also saw several blacksmith's hammers. They were made to pound steel shoes into shape, maybe they would be used to pound apart handcuffs.

"How are you going to swing the hammer, dummy, assuming you can even get a hold of it? First thing, you need to get those hands in front of you before you can do anything. Now, how to do that?"

It took a bit of a struggle, but I was finally able to stand up. I bent over as far as I could and slid my wrists down past my bottom, the cuffs biting into my skin.

Okay. Now I was bent over with my hands behind my legs. The next step would be to somehow get my feet up and over the cuffs. I decided that would work best if I was lying on my side and I shuffled back over toward the cot.

The sound of a car engine stopped me. If this was Phil coming back and he found me like this things could get even uglier. I clenched my teeth, then pulled my wrists up back behind my back. I sat down on the cot.

"I decided to be nice. I need you alive for the time being, anyway," Phil said, coming in the door. "Here's a cup of water and a milkshake. There's a bowl on the floor you can use for a toilet."

He pulled me to my feet again. "I'll just fasten this here." He undid my right wrist and fastened the handcuff that was still attached to my left arm to a piece of chain attached to a ring in the wall. "This is in the wood good and tight, so don't bother to pull on it," he said. "Now, I got your boyfriend on the line. You tell him to go and get that quilt and we'll call him back in the morning."

I could here Rick's voice coming out of the cell phone Phil held up to my ear. "Maggie, is that you? Are you okay? Where are you?"

I had to swallow a couple of times to get my voice to work. "Rick, yes, I'm okay. Phil wants that quilt, but I told him we gave it to Marty. I know it will take you some time to get it back."

"But …" he said. I didn't let him go on.

"Time, I know, Rick, it will take some time." Let him understand me, I begged silently.

For a minute Rick was quiet. Then he said, "Yes, you are right. It will take time. I will do what I can tonight. Tell that bastard to call me tomorrow."

Phil grabbed the phone. "That's enough. Listen Rick, you get going on this. I want that quilt by tomorrow or you get your Maggie back in bits and pieces, understand?"

I don't know what Rick said, but Phil's face flamed. "Same to you, hot shot," he said and cut the connection.

"I'll see you tomorrow," he said, and walked out. The car door slammed and I waited for the car engine to start. I listened as hard as I could, but heard nothing after the sound of the door. Phil must be planning on spending the night in the car so he could guard the stable. Didn't matter, though, because I was going to get out, I was determined. I would have to get out, and soon.

CHAPTER 58

▼

Rick understood that I needed some time. I knew that no way would Phil let me live after he had the quilt. He knew I would be more than willing to testify against him again and he couldn't risk that. I was as good as dead once the quilt was in Phil's hands. I had to find a way to get away before that happened. I needed to escape.

Phil had done me a huge favor, although he wasn't smart enough to see it. With one hand free I could work on getting the handcuffs off. I looked at the horseshoeing tools. The hammers were out, if I started pounding on the cuffs he would hear me. But, the hoof nippers were a possibility.

I looked at the handcuffs. Typical for Phil, he took the cheap way out. It looked like he bought them at an adult book store that sold sex toys. They were meant to restrain, but they were made out of lightweight stamped metal and were not the sturdy police issue type. Hopefully they would be somewhat easy to break. Phil was right, though. The ring with the short piece of chain that he fastened my one hand to was very securely set into the wood. Without some sort of hefty tool that ring would not be coming out. The handcuff chain was my best bet. At least the ring was mounted in the wall at about waist height. It may have been used as a hitching device for horses, but its being low rather than high would make it easier for me to work at cutting the handcuffs.

I had to lie down on the floor and use my feet, but I was finally able to get a hold of the hoof nippers. Horses' hooves can be as hard as a rock, so these nippers were pretty tough. I hoped they would be up to the task of cutting the handcuff metal.

Before I started, I worked on the milkshake for a few minutes. I hadn't eaten in hours and was starting to feel shaky. If I were going to get away I would need some energy.

After what seemed like an endless struggle, the nippers were in my hand. Now, to figure out how to use them one-handed. I was going to have to somehow get them clipped on the chain connecting the handcuffs together, then lean on the handles to make them cut.

I worked until exhaustion took over. Every time I got the nippers over the chain and I tried to make the cut, they slipped. Finally, I gave up. I pushed the nippers out of sight under the cot and looked up at the windows. While I struggled night had come; the glass was black.

"I'll rest a bit then try again," I said. "I just can't do anymore right now."

I laid down, not expecting to sleep. But, almost as soon as my head hit the lumpy wad of burlap that served as a pillow, I was out.

CHAPTER 59

▼

I awoke with a start. Where was I? When I sat up and tried to move my left arm, I remembered. That was the hand that was still cuffed to the ring in the wall in this old horse stable. The hoof nippers. Was I up to trying them again? The windows were still dark, maybe I had enough time left.

I groped under the cot, trying not to think about what critters might be sharing the space with me. With the nippers in hand again, I went back to work.

This time I tried bracing them against the wood where the ring was secured, then maneuvering the handcuff chain into the nippers. This seemed to give me a little better control.

There, the chain was in the nippers. "Now, be careful," I said, "Just go slow and cut those cuffs." I held one end of the long nipper handles and carefully leaned on the other one. The jaws bit down on the chain and held. I leaned against the handle, praying the nippers were tough enough to cut the handcuff chain.

I could see the jaws digging into the metal when something slipped. The nippers crashed to the floor, sounding like a sonic boom.

I kicked them under cot and lay down, fighting to feign sleep. I waited for an eternity, but nothing happened. Phil must not have heard the noise.

Exhaling a breath I didn't realized I was holding, I felt under the cot for the nippers. I had to try again.

This time I tried to get the nippers as square with the wood as I could. That way, when I started to push on them they shouldn't skew off to one side. After several near misses, I once again the handcuff chain was in the jaws of the nippers. I took a deep breath and held it.

I leaned against the nippers. They started to slide, so I stopped and tried to get them in a better position. I leaned on them again. This time they felt solid. I turned my body to get as square with the wall as I could. I used my left forearm across my upper abdomen to push on the nipper handle. I hoped this way I could get better leverage. I was also able to hold on to one of the nipper handles with my left hand this way, too. I started to push again.

Sweat popped out on my face. The nippers seemed to be making some progress through the metal, but I just couldn't get enough push on them. I kicked my shoes off. Maybe I could get a little more traction on the floor. I pushed again. It felt like my arm was going to meet my backbone soon. I stopped to take a breath.

"This may not work," I mumbled, "But, it has to!"

I wondered what time it was. It must be still be night, as the windows were still black. I didn't know if I had slept for an hour or a minute, though, so I had no idea how close to morning it was. Nighttime would make escaping easier, so I had to get out of here while it was still dark. I just HAD to.

I repositioned by arm against the nipper handle. There was a long, painful groove down my arm; if I got out of here I would have some interesting bruises. Okay, now, DO this.

Again I filled my lungs, then held my breath. PUSH, push. I felt the nippers give and nearly wept; they probably slipped off the chain again. Then I took a look at the chain. Wow! One link of the chain was cut through!

The nipper's jaws were fat enough that they spread the cut ends of the link apart just far enough to allow me to pull another link through the gap. I was free, at least free in this building. I'd be wearing a tin bracelet for awhile, but that I could stand. Now, to figure out how to get outside.

I sat down on the cot for a minute and drank the rest of the milkshake. It was a thin liquid by now and it went down fast. I could feel the sugar moving into my quivering muscles and it felt good. I looked around the stable, invigorated. I would get out now.

There was a small hay loft overhead. Bucking bales up a ladder to store them would not have been any fun. That's why in most upper haylofts like this there was an outside door to allow the hay to be loaded into the loft from a conveyor belt or a hoist of some kind. That could be my best bet.

I put my shoes back on and scrambled up the ladder to the hay loft. Yes! There was a door in the end of the building. It was held shut on the inside with a simple nail slid through a hasp. No need to worry about somebody getting in up on the upper level like that. I opened the door.

CHAPTER 60

▼

The ground looked very far away in the faint moonlight. I might be out, but I am still not away. I couldn't see Phil's car from this side, he must be around on the opposite side of the building. That was good. I realized, too, that the steady sound I was hearing was water. Now I looked around a little. Suddenly I knew where I was.

There is a pasture on the south side of Trent just a little ways east of Pines Road. For more years than I could remember, two horses lived in that pasture. There is a paved road that runs across the pasture and down to the little stable and hay barn. There used to be hay piled against one side of the building, too. I always looked for those horses whenever I went by here. They seemed very content, they had each other and all the grass and hay they wanted. Their owners tended to them, too, I could tell. The water trough was always full and in the winter there was a heater in it. The horses looked healthy, too, their coats glossy and hooves tended to.

The horses had been gone from this place for awhile, though. I couldn't remember the last time I had seen them here and I didn't know what happened to them. They were in another good place, I hoped. Now I also wondered if there was still hay piled against the outside of the stable. If there was, I might be able to get down that way. Otherwise I was still trapped. This was too high to jump and there was nothing I could use to climb down the side of the building, just a ledge running across the tops of the door below.

I stepped out onto the ledge. My stomach tensed, this was really scary. It had rained earlier, but it stopped some time ago and the roof looked fairly dry. One slip and I was toast. Crablike, I inched my way across to the corner of the roof.

Once up on the roof I felt somewhat more secure, but I was still a long way from the ground and getting away. Even inside my shoes it felt like my toes were clenching onto the prickly shingles on the roof of the stable. I inched about half-way down the length of the building and peeked over the eave. No hay, but I could see Phil's car. I took another deep breath and went back the way I had come.

I looked at two more sides of the building without success. If there was nothing to break my fall on the fourth side I would have to figure something else out. I walked to the edge of the roof again, crossed my fingers and said a small prayer; this was my last chance.

Hooray! There was still some hay piled by the side of the building. Not a lot, but maybe enough to break my fall. I worked my way to the edge.

The people who built this stable put a gutter on this edge of the roof, probably to keep water running off the roof from pouring down on the hay. I decided rather than just slide off the roof and drop, or jump, I would try to hang by my hands from the gutter. My fall would then be that much shorter. I laid down on the roof and wiggled my way to the edge.

I reached out and pushed down the gutter as hard as I could. It appeared to be securely fastened to the roof edge. I wasn't sure how I was going to get myself over the edge without just plunging to the ground, though. I laid on the roof for a minute, thinking.

Finally, I decided to just start by easing my feet over the edge and hopefully the rough shakes on the roof would keep me from sliding too fast. I turned over on my stomach and began inching to the edge.

A fit of the giggles stopped me. I was close to hysteria, that I could tell. But, I knew what these giggles could do; reduce me to a muscleless blob. Once when my sister and I were out for a walk she caught her foot in an exposed tree root. She fell forward, ending up bent at the middle with her hands on the ground out in front of her. She was helpless in this position and could not move a muscle, except for her those in her jaw.

"Give me your hand and help me up," she yelled. "My ankle feels like its about to break."

I held out my hand, but it was useful as a piece of cooked spaghetti. I could no more grip her hand and help her stand up than fly. But, I could sure giggle. She had to talk very sternly to me to get me sobered up enough to help her. I still get needled about that day occasionally.

Now here I was, giggling away. Even worse, though I had used Phil's make-shift toilet before going up into the loft, my bladder felt like it was about to burst. There was nothing I could do but wait this episode out.

Finally, the giggles subsided. I lay for a moment on the shake roof, begging my body to respond. Again I worked myself to the edge of the roof. The shingles were impeding my progress, but that was a good thing. I knew that once my waist hit the gutter I would lose that advantage. When my upper body started over the edge I would be lifted away from the stickery shakes and I was afraid I would slide right off.

"Okay, stop," I whispered. The bottom half of me was dangling in space and the shingles were keeping me in place. But, staying here did me no good. "This is it, do or die," I muttered.

I reached down and took a hold of the edge of the gutter. My arm strength was good, but I didn't know if there was enough muscle there to hold me. I wiggled and squirmed to let the top half of me slide over the edge.

The slide started slow, then faster. I tried with all my might to let my arms bend slowly, gradually lowering me to the gutter. The last few inches were fast though, and I tried to concentrate on keeping my grip on the edge of the gutter.

Suddenly I was hanging in space. My fingers had held onto the edge of the gutter. I peered down. The pile of hay still looked a long ways away, but I would have to just go for it. Soon, too. I could feel my fingers starting to slip off the smooth gutter edge. I closed my eyes and let go.

CHAPTER 61

▼

I do not like to fly; I do not like being up off the ground with nothing under my feet. Tall buildings, edges of cliffs, and other high places don't bother me; I was still standing on something. But up in an airplane, or a parasail, or, Lord forbid, a hang glider? No, thank you. I have this fear of not being able to get down. Irrational, I knew, but there it is.

I got down, though. It only took a split second from the time I let go of the gutter until my feet slammed into the pile of hay, but it seemed like forever. Then I was on the ground and buried in damp, musty hay.

The wind was knocked out of me and I lay for a few seconds until my diaphragm remembered how to work. That first breath, laced as it was with dust and mold, was delightful. The landing was a terrific jolt, but the hay pretty much cushioned me from hitting the ground too hard. Nothing seemed to hurt; now to see if everything still worked.

I slid off the hay pile and gingerly stood up. I felt sore all over, but my ankles and knees seemed fine. I took a tentative step. My legs shook, but they held me up. That was okay, too. Now I could get away from here.

The sound of water had stuck in the back of my mind ever since I opened the loft door. Once I figured out where that water sound was coming from I knew exactly where I was. The Spokane River was nearby; I remembered now that the pasture fence ran down to the bank. Trent Road was not that far away, though. I would just sneak past Phil's car and walk back up the road to Trent and find some help.

CHAPTER 62

▼

So far, so good. I could see the barbed wire fence and gate that closed off the road. That would be simple to climb through—it was a standard three-strand fence of barbed wire and the wire usually has plenty of flex it in. I had stepped through fences like this a lot, not only as a child, but when going on farm calls with Brad Mancusco and Rick.

The windshield of Phil's car was misted from his breathing and I could not see him; he must be in the back seat. That tinting that kept me from looking out shielded me now. Phil would not be able to see me. Even so, I bent double to walk past the car.

I was just a few feet from the fence when my feet started to tingle. Then I felt the hairs on my arms stand up. I stopped walking and waited for the clouds to blow past the moon again.

"Shit," I whispered, "He's hot wired the whole fence."

I felt like I was in one of the frustrating movies where the good guys have to overcome endless obstacles and ALMOST get away then there is ONE MORE THING they have to conquer. And here it is, hot wire.

Lots of large animal owners strung a single line of bare wire around the inside of their fences if they were using barbed wire or a wood fence. This is called hot wire because it is electrified. The animals quickly learn if they try to get through the fence, or get close enough to chew a wood fence, that they will get a shock. It's not a huge shock, but unpleasant. I had accidentally zapped myself a couple of times and I didn't like the sensation. The piece of wire is fastened to the fence posts with insulators so that the whole fence isn't electrified. There is also a place, usually at a gate, where the ends of the wire are connected with a loop and a hook arrangement. The hook part has a plastic handle that is used to disconnect the wire and break the current when people have to get in and out of the fenced area.

This field is fenced in barbed wire and the flash of moonlight showed me that Phil had taken the hot wire and fastened it directly to the barbed wire, effectively charging the whole fence. Because the fence posts, indeed everything, was wet from the rain, the current flowed through all the wires and some even through the ground, where I was feeling it.. If I had insulated wire cutters I could have snipped the hot wire, breaking the circuit, but I didn't have any. He had taken the plastic handle off the wire across the gate, too, so that was out. There was no way to get through the fence without touching the wire. The shock would be unpleasant, assuming he was using a regular electric fence current. But, if he had hooked it up some other way, well, the jolt could be lethal. I would have to find another way out of the pasture.

I sighed. Maybe it would be easier to just wait by the car until he came out and then hit him over the head, or something. I laughed a bit at myself. "Probably end up hitting yourself in the leg. Might as well go walk the fence."

About halfway down one side of the fence I was stopped by thick brush. Walking around it brought me out into the middle of the pasture and it was too dark to see where the fence went. Blundering into it in the dark would be bad. I decided to walk down the middle of the pasture toward the river.

As I got closer to the river I noticed a gap in the tall grass. It was a dry stream bed curving down the slope toward the river. There was no water in the stream now. Even with the recent rain it remained empty, until the snow pack in the mountains melted this stream would not exist. The river level was low, too. If I could get under the fence where it ran down to the river I could walk along the bank until I could get up onto the road. This would take a lot longer that just hiking up the pasture to Trent Road, but it also might be safer if Phil discovered I had gotten out and he came looking for me.

I followed the stream bed toward the river. The air got colder as I got closer to the water; a walk on the beach would not be pleasant tonight.

When there was water in the stream bed it flowed fast down to the river and dug a fairly deep channel. That will give me enough room to slide under the wire, I thought. I laid down again. "Seems all my escapes involve lying down," I muttered. "Well, here goes."

Face up and feet first I inched my way under the fence. I could feel the electric current jittering down on my skin. It felt like it took forever to work my body under the fence but at least I was going downhill. I finally I saw the wire go past my eyes.

My feet were in the river by the time my head passed under the wire and I was able to roll over and stand up. The water was so cold it felt like a thousand needles on my skin, but oddly refreshing at the same time.

I looked around. As I hoped, the water was low enough that there was river bank exposed that I could walk on. It would be long hike. The first place that I could picture that I had a hope of getting up to the road would be at Plantes Ferry Park on Upriver Drive. This was a spot where Native Americans and other explorers forded the river. The banks were not so steep there and there were houses nearby, too. I should be able to get some help.

I had only gone a little ways when I heard yelling. It sounded like Phil, damn, he must have awakened and found out that I escaped from the stable. I started to run.

CHAPTER 63

▼

Trying to run on the rocky stream bed was not easy. The glaciers that gouged out this valley and river channel pushed rocks before them for hundreds of miles. As those rocks were moved along any sharp corners were scraped off until the rocks were round and smooth, ideal for building the many rock walls still in scattered places throughout the valley, but also perfect for slipping on. With visions of broken ankles dancing before me I tried to hurry carefully.

Branches from the bushes growing along the water grabbed at me with prickly hands as I went by, but they failed to stop me. I kept up my stumbling running until the stitch in my side forced me to slow down.

I heard yelling coming from behind me. Phil was coming after me for sure. He also must have turned the power off to the fence because I heard him climbing through the wire, the pinging sounds coming clearly to me. He was heading down the riverbank in my direction. Noise travels so well at night and over the water and he sounded like he was right next to me. I hoped that because he was also cursing and shouting as he ran that he wouldn't be able to hear me, too. Now he would catch me, though, unless I could hide.

My lungs felt seared by the cold, wet, air. I had to struggle to breathe slowly and carefully, otherwise I panted like a steam engine. I worked my way around a bridge support column for the Burlington Northern-Santa Fe Railroad tracks that crossed the river high overhead. I was thrilled to find that on the other side the brush grew down almost to the water's edge.

I started to wiggle my way into the brush when a crashing sound behind me made me stop short. A bear. All I could think about that there was a bear in the bushes with me and that I would end up as an ursine breakfast. I froze, trying not to breathe at all. The brush rustled again and for an instant I was eyeball to eyeball with a small buck. He looked like a mule deer, from the size of his ears.

I'm not sure who was more startled, me or the deer, but the deer decided to be the one to panic and run away. With one bound he was up the bank and away. I let my breath out with a sigh. No bear, thank heaven, but now I could feel those giggles of stress bubbling up again. I fought to suppress them; the noise would give me away for sure.

Stuffing the edge of my hand in my mouth I bit down. I closed my eyes and held my breath until the river sound became a roaring in my ears, drowning out every other sound.

Pain finally overcame laughter. I opened my eyes and took a careful breath. My ears were working normally again. I hunkered down in the bushes. I could hear Phil coming my way, crashing along the bank and cursing, but I couldn't see a thing. I stayed as still as I could, praying that a spider or something wouldn't pick that minute to slither down my shirt.

Then from behind my leafy fortress I could see Phil come out from behind the concrete support and stop. "This was a waste of time," I heard him say, panting. "She wouldn't have the guts to come this far. Might as well go get the car and go up to Trent. Stupid bitch is probably up there trying to hitch a ride." I heard Phil's shoes clattering on the rocks as he moved away from me.

I waited. If he was trying a trick he would be standing on the other side of the support, waiting for me to make a move. I counted to a hundred. Then I still did not move, afraid. The BNSF solved my dilemma about then. A freight train came onto the trestle, filling the night with noise and shaking the ground. I took a chance and fought my way out of the bushes.

I was stiff and sore from standing still, but as least my respiratory rate and heart rate had settled down. I headed downstream again, hoping the train was a good long one.

Phil must have gone back to the pasture, as after the train was gone all I could hear were my own footsteps and the sound of the river. I plodded on.

There is a sliver of light in the east when I finally get to Plantes Ferry Park. I am damp all the way into to my bones and shivering with cold. My feet feel like blocks of ice and I stumble often before I find the spot where the bank became a more gentle slope towards Upriver Drive. I concentrated on putting one foot in front of the other, working my way up to the road. I had always liked the house that sat by the side of the road overlooking the water. Now I just hoped the people that lived there wanted to be a friend to man, living in that house by the side of the road. I staggered up the driveway towards the front porch.

A light came on just as I put my foot on the bottom step. Thank goodness I wouldn't have to try and get somebody out of bed. This time of the year the sun comes up around six-thirty; that isn't too early, anyway.

The front door opened and a woman reached out to get the paper. She about jumped out her skin when she saw me and I wondered just how bedraggled I looked.

"Can you help me?" I managed to croak.

Within seconds I am wrapped in a thick terry cloth robe and seated in front of a fire roaring in a wood stove. My feet are thawing out in a pan of warm water and there is a cup of hot cocoa in my hand. If there is a heaven, I thought, this must be it.

The woman, her husband, and two children were sitting at the kitchen table, trying to keep their interest on their breakfasts. I had yet to say a word beyond "thank you" to the woman who took me to a bathroom, gave me the robe, then told me to hand out my wet clothes and take a hot shower. My clothes went in the dryer and as soon as I came out of the bathroom she led me to the chair in front of the stove.

"Can you tell us what happened?" the man said. "You look like you've spent the night in the woods."

"It's a long story," I said, "But here're the high points. My ex-husband, who was in prison, escaped. I have something he wants and he kidnapped me to try and force me to give it to him. He locked me up in a small horse barn just east of Pines Road, but I managed to get out and walked down the river to escape."

"You came all that way in the dark?" said the woman, looking out the window where it was not yet full daylight. "I don't know how you did it."

I shook my head. "I'm not too sure either; I just kept putting one foot in front of the other until I got to Plantes Ferry Park."

The little boy was very shy, but in a tiny whisper he had to ask, "Weren't you scared?"

"I sure was," I said, then thought about the "bear." I couldn't help it, the giggles came. This time I gave in to them and laughed until tears ran down my face. When I was finally able to pick up my head from where I let it drop to the back of the chair, the family was looking at me with genuine alarm. They were sure they had a lunatic in their midst, I was certain.

I took a hiccupping breath. "Sorry about that. You must think I'm crazy, but there was this deer ..." I had to laugh again and after I told them the story they laughed too, relieved.

"You saved my life this morning, you really did. I can't thank you enough. Now, if you'll let me make a couple of phone calls I can get out of your way."

CHAPTER 64

▼

I learned that the kids were Alex and Cindy and the dad of the family, whom I now knew was Roger Swenson and his wife, Brenda, would have none of it.

"You just tell me where you need to go and I'll take you there," Roger said. "Besides, I want to hear more of this story."

"I don't want to put you out any more than I already have," I said. "I can just call …"

"Don't be silly," said Brenda. "It's Saturday and Roger does not have to go to work. He'll be glad to escape some of the Saturday chores." She handed me my dry clothes. "Go put these back on and I'll fix you a plate of food while you get dressed. You have to be hungry by now."

Never had plain scrambled eggs, bacon, hash browns, and white toast tasted so wonderful. I hadn't realized how hungry I was until I took the first bite. It was all I could to not to lick the plate when I was done. Alex and Cindy were out of their jammies now. Their faces solemn, they watched me eat every bite. I'm sure they thought I was some outer space alien, or something. Their eyes followed my cocoa cup as I took the last sip.

"That was wonderful, Brenda. Now I better get out of your hair."

Roger stood up. "My truck's around on the side. I'm ready whenever you are."

"Are you sure?" I said, "I can call somebody …"

"It's not a problem at all. Like I said, I hope to hear more of this story of yours."

"Okay," I said. "I'm ready, too. "'Bye Cindy, 'bye Alex. It was nice to meet you."

Cindy smiled a bit at this and waved her hand. Alex just continued to stare. This family will be discussing my Saturday morning invasion for a while, I thought.

Roger pulled stopped his pickup at the end of the driveway. I started to climb in, but Roger stopped me. "What's this? Handcuffs?"

"Good grief," I said, holding up my arm and peering at it. "That has been there so long I'd almost stopped noticing it. Yeah, this is half of a pair, anyway. The rest is still hanging in the stable."

"Just a minute," Roger said and went into the garage. He came back with a pair of bolt cutters. "This ought to do it," he said, and applied the cutters. Seconds later the handcuff half was on the ground.

"Thanks," I said, rubbing my sore wrist. I bent down and picked up the twisted piece of metal. "The sheriff may want this," I said. Roger and I both got into the truck.

"Which way?" he said.

"I think I'll just have you take me back to the animal hospital where I work," I said, pointing to the east. "My car should still be there. It's just a little ways further out on Trent; that won't put you too much out of your way."

Roger took Upriver Drive to McDonald Road and turned south to get to Trent. Then it was just a quick trip to the clinic. I told him a bit more about what had happened to me over the last twenty-four hours, which seemed more like twenty-four days. By the time he pulled into the parking lot at All Animals Hospital and Crematorium, he was ready to go after Phil himself. I was relieved to see the Blazer where I had left it; had it only been the day before? I was also puzzled, but glad, to see Rick's truck parked in the back. I knew Jeanne was on call for the weekend and wondered why he was here. Maybe there was a particular animal he wanted to check up on; he had done that before, or possibly an emergency call that came to him because Jeanne was already busy.

"Here's our phone number," Roger said, tearing a piece of paper off a note pad that was attached to the truck's dashboard. "If you need anything, please call us."

"Thank you, Roger. You and Brenda have been wonderful. My purse is inside. Please wait a minute, I want to pay you for all your trouble."

"Don't even talk like that," Roger said. "It's been no trouble at all. Now, you take care of yourself and call if you need anything." He jumped out of the truck and opened the door for me. "It's been nice meeting you, Maggie."

"You, too, Roger. Thanks again and thank Brenda again for me, will you?"

With a nod and a grin, he hopped back into his truck and drove off. I smiled. I had taken a peek into his and Brenda's bedroom and noted the cream, green, and maroon color scheme. Cindy had been wearing pj's with Barbie on them and Alex's were decorated with trucks. I knew the colors and themes for three quilts. No way could I let the help they gave me today go unrewarded.

Now, to go in and see why Rick was at the clinic on a Saturday when he was not on call.

CHAPTER 65

▼

The front door was locked, but my keys had survived the night with me. I pulled them out, but before I opened the door I noticed that one of the small windows that surrounded the door looked like it was punched out. Hmm. I wonder what that is all about, I thought as I opened the door and walked in.

Rick was sitting at my desk, his head in his hands. Marty Adams was standing next to him, looking furious. They both looked up at the sound of the door opening.

I don't know who looked the most astonished. For a second nobody spoke.

"Hi," I said.

Rick leaped to his feet and rushed around the desk. He grabbed me so hard he nearly knocked me off my feet. He buried his face behind my left ear and I could feel him shuddering; the poor man was in tears.

He pulled his face back to look at me. "It really is you," he said, his voice tremulous. "My God, Maggie, I thought I had lost you."

By now I was in tears myself. "No, It's me. What are you guys doing here, anyway?"

Rick buried his face in my shoulder again. I looked at Marty. "You gonna tell me, or what?"

Marty's voice was shaky, too. "Phil called Rick at home this morning. He told him you were tied to a bridge support in the river; he refused to say exactly where. We had until nine o'clock to call him back with the news that we had his quilt and he would tell us where you were. If we didn't call on time," Marty pointed to the clock, it read 9:15, "He said he would leave the area and not tell us where to find you. With as cold as the water is, we knew if we couldn't find you right away that you would die of hypothermia. Rick knew the quilt here in the office somewhere, but we couldn't find it. I just put a full-scale search in place … I need to call them back and cancel that." He grabbed the phone and started to punch in numbers.

"You look like hell," Rick said, "What happened, anyway?"

I looked down at my clothes. They were dry, but filthy. I knew from the Swenson's mirror what my hair looked like, too. "You don't like my new look? I think it's rather stylish, myself."

"Enough, you two," said Marty, dropping the phone back in it cradle. "At least I was able to get the search canceled before they mobilized all the troops. Maggie, we need to know where Phil was holding you so we can go look for him. Where were you all this time?"

I told Marty about the abandoned horse stable in the field off Trent. He picked the phone up again and started to chatter into it. Rick had not let go of me, but I needed to sit down. I dropped with a sigh of relief into a waiting room chair, Rick next to me. I told him the story up to when I got to the Swenson's house and I saw the anger growing in his eyes. Marty came over to us before Rick could say anything.

"I rode over with Rick, but I have a car coming to pick me up," he said. "Are you two going home pretty soon?"

"Just as soon as your ride gets here," I said. "I need to get out of these filthy clothes and take another shower. I need to tell you about the Swenson's, too." I said to Rick.

"Okay," said Marty, "But stay alert. Phil might try to grab you again, Maggie."

"Don't worry about that," Rick said. "If that two-bit hoodlum even shows his stupid face around us I'll…."

"You'll what, you panty-waist little boy?"

I always wondered about the phrase, 'my blood ran cold.' Now I knew what it meant; my whole body felt like it turned to ice at the sound of Phil's voice. I couldn't believe he managed to just waltz in the door without any of us hearing him, but we had all been a bit distracted. Now here was evil staring me in the face again. I didn't know if I had any reserves left. I wished I could faint on demand, but I had never managed to do that. Now I would have in a heartbeat, anything to not know what was coming next.

"I figured our Maggie here would come back for her car … that's how stupid she is," Phil said. He pushed his way the rest of the way into the waiting room, a pistol filling his hand. "And who's this new guy, you got two boyfriends now, you whore?"

Marty was standing stock still. I knew he had a gun, too, but there was no way he could chance going for it.

"You're boyfriend number two," Phil said, pointing at Marty and sneering, "Ha! boyfriend number two, that's pretty funny, another piece of shit for you, bitch. That's okay, now you'll have two deaths on your conscience, at least until you are dead, too. You see, I don't need any of you people any more. I know where my money is, thanks to that fat cow Barbara."

I must have looked boggled, because Phil laughed, not a pleasant sound. "Yeah, she sent me a note spilling her guts. She didn't know how to send it to the prison, so she sent it to Stub. Barbara's note told me where the money is. She was afraid I wouldn't be able to figure out the code she put on the quilt. Now, I just need to go there and talk them into letting me into the lock box. Shouldn't be too hard, Barbara fixed it so either one of us can get in. They'll have my signature on file and they'll give me my property when I say I've lost the key. Stub's coming to join the party, by the way. He should be here any minute. He's mad that you guys tried to use him to fool me."

"Your property," I said, putting as much disgust as I could into my voice. If only Marty's ride would get here, I thought. The longer Phil talked, the better. "You are nothing but a common thief, that's all you are, and you hit women to get your way. You're a pathetic loser, too."

"You lose this time," he said. "I'm not going to be fooled into letting that bug me so that this brave-looking boyfriend number two can try and jump me. Besides which, I am an uncommon thief. Let's see, I think I'll get started here with boyfriend number two."

"So if you know where the money is, what are you doing here, Phil?" Marty said. "You don't need the quilt any more, after all. Why don't you just leave before you do something that could cost you the rest of your life on death row?"

Phil sneered again. "Oh, you are real smart, aren't you. You just want to figure out the code on the quilt yourself and then you will know where to start looking for me, or maybe take the cash for yourself, asshole. That's not gonna happen. If I don't have the quilt, I can't take the chance that you do. Once you losers are dead I won't care about that fucking quilt. It won't mean anything to anybody else."

I saw Phil raise his gun higher and take aim at Marty. I squeezed my eyes shut and felt Rick tense up next to me.

CHAPTER 66

▼

BOOM! It sounded like a cannon had gone off in the clinic. But, just before the boom I thought I heard glass breaking. I couldn't help it, I opened my eyes.

Marty was back at my desk, the phone in his hand again. My ears were ringing so loudly that I couldn't hear what he was saying. Phil was on the floor, a widening pool of blood underneath him. He was groaning and thrashing, probably from the weight of the deputy who was kneeling on his chest. The gun Phil had pointed at Marty was on the floor out of his reach.

"Hold still, sir," I heard the deputy say. "An ambulance is on the way."

I realized I had a death grip on Rick's hand. "What happened," I managed to say.

"I'm not sure," he said. "It looked like Phil was just about to shoot Marty when somebody, must've been the deputy there, came slamming through the door and fired at Phil. I think we have him to thank for saving us all."

Marty came out from behind my desk and leaned down next to Phil. "Just a flesh wound, you creep," he said. "They'll get you stitched up in the ER and then it's off to jail for you. You'll be spending a long time in prison, too. With the kidnapping of Maggie the feds are involved now, so you'll be doing a lot of hard time."

Phil could only moan. Darn it, the bleeding had stopped. I could see where Marty had ripped Phil's shirt away. There was a deep furrow across Phil's shoulder where the bullet had grazed him. Good. I was glad he wasn't dead; I wanted him to suffer for as many years as possible.

Marty dug through Phil's pockets. "Nothing," he said. "Where's the note, Phil?"

"Fuck you," said Phil, attempting to spit at Marty. You will never find that money."

"Oh, yes, we will," I said. I pulled myself away from Rick and went over to the spot under the ceiling tile where the quilt was hidden. I climbed up on a chair and pushed the tile up and pulled the quilt down. "Here is your precious quilt," I said, "And I know how to figure out where the money is, too."

Rick groaned. "I can't believe I forgot about that hiding place. I could have prevented this whole thing …"

"Shhhh," I cut him off. "I'm glad you forgot. No way would I have wanted you to give Phil this quilt."

From the floor Phil roared like a furious lion and tried to leap to his feet. But Marty was holding his chest down and the other deputy put hobbles around Phil's ankles, so all he could do was thrash around like a fish out of water.

"To paraphrase you, you lose this time." I said. It was all I could do to keep from delivering a swift kick to Phil's ribs.

Through the now-shattered front door of the clinic, I saw the ambulance as it pulled up out in front. I watched them load Phil onto a gurney, Marty and the other deputy making sure his ankle hobbles and handcuffs were securely fastened to the side rails. The deputy who saved our lives, I didn't even catch his name, climbed into the ambulance. Spokane County lawmen were not going to let Phil to escape on their watch.

I watched the ambulance until it disappeared around a curve in Trent Road. I went back into the clinic.

"Oh, my God," I said, "I just thought of something. Phil said Stub was coming here, too. I don't think I could face another gun today." Now the tears I had been holding back came in earnest and I sobbed like a baby. Marty came over and put his arm around me.

"It's okay, Maggie. We knew about Stub and have been looking for him. One of our deputy's made a routine traffic stop this morning and luckily he ran the driver's license and figured out who it was before he wrote him a ticket and let him go. Stub's being detained for now."

CHAPTER 67

▼

Rick was mopping up the last traces of Phil's blood off the marble floor. Marty was sitting in my desk chair again, head back, eyes closed. I knew he had miles of paperwork to do on this and he looked worn out.

"You okay, Marty?" I said.

"Yeah," he said, without opening his eyes. "Just a little shaky, that's all. Looking down the barrel of a gun is never a fun thing. I gotta tell you, it looks like a cannon is pointed in your face. That stuff about your life flashing before your eyes? Doesn't happen to me; I'm too busy trying to hold down the terror and figure out what to do. I didn't think we'd make it this time. Thank God for Aaron Christenson."

"I wondered what his name was," I said. "I think I need to make him a quilt."

Marty smiled. "Or at least a batch of cookies."

"No way! He'd be lucky to get one cookie; I know you guys."

Marty sat up, a tinge of color back in his face. "You're probably right. Hey, I don't know about you two, but I'm starving. Aaron left his cruiser here for me. I'm going to run down to Pizza Pipeline there in Millwood and get us some pizza." Before Rick or I could respond, Marty was out the door and down the road.

"Whew," said Rick. "What a morning. This makes that drug business with Lynda Mancusco seem like a walk in the park."

"Yeah, this was even worse than hiding under that old rowboat on the beach in Ilwaco. At least I didn't have to go swimming this time, just a lot of wading, and man, was that water ever cold."

Rick sat and listened while I told him the rest of what the last twenty-four hours had been like for me. His expressions ran the gamut: angry, frightened, relieved, and angry again. But, Phil was gone again, hopefully this time for good. I'd be called to testify in court again, but that would be a pleasure. He'd plead innocent, that I knew. A long time ago I figured out that Phil was a sociopath; the rest of society's rules and regulations, not to mention mores, had nothing to do with him. He was always right and his way was always the right way, no matter who else suffered.

When I was done with my story, Rick got up and went over to look at the front door. "After Marty gets back I better go get some stuff to secure this door until Monday," he said. "This door is never going to close again in its present condition."

"I'll give Georgia a call," I said. "She can go up and feed the cats and let Brandy out. That way I can help you."

"You're exhausted, sweetie," Rick said. "You go on home; I can take care of this."

"And who will protect the place while you're off getting supplies? I can go upstairs and lie down if I feel the need. Besides, I'd feel safer here for the time being."

When All Animals Hospital and Crematory was the Hennessey funeral home and crematorium, the employees took turns spending the night in the building. They needed to have someone who could answer the phone and go out on any after-hours calls. Some people wanted to start making arrangements immediately, too, so someone to help them needed to be available. The apartment above the waiting room is basically just a bed, toilet, sink, shower, and microwave, but it had come in handy on several occasions for us. If there is a critically ill animal in the clinic, one of the doctors can stay there and get up to check on the animal without having to make the drive from home. Again today the apartment could prove useful, should I need it. For now, though, I wasn't tired, although I knew when the crash came it would be a big one.

"Well, okay, if you're sure," Rick said. "Look, here comes Marty."

Marty staggered in the door, clutching three huge pizza boxes. "I got three of the biggest ones they had," he said. "Maggie, would you get the drinks out of my car, please?"

Four liters of pop should do it, I thought, hefting the bulging bag from Marty's front seat. I took the pop in and went to the back of the clinic and got some paper cups. For a few minutes the only sounds were of pizza being chewed and washed down with pop. I still had Brenda's great breakfast on board, but I was unable to resist a slice of Italian sausage pizza. In the middle of a bite I remembered Jeanne.

"Jeanne! Is she okay? Did Phil hurt her? What happened to her yesterday anyway?"

"Whoa," said Rick, "One question at a time! Yes, Jeanne is fine. Phil came up behind her as she was unlocking the back door and pushed his way in behind her. All he did was lock her in one of the kennel rooms and the first client of the day let her out. She figured out that Phil had taken you and she called the sheriff right away, but of course we had no clue where he had taken you. She is very disgusted with herself that she didn't see his car parked in the back; she said she was thinking about a sick cat that had her worried. Phil had a quite a lead on us and we just had to wait until he called, and of course, you know the rest of it."

Marty ate until I thought he would burst, then left to go to his office. He told me he usually wished he didn't have to work on Saturday, but today he wasn't going to mind spending the time documenting all of Phil's crimes. I would have to stop by the office on Monday and give a formal statement, he said, but if I sat down in the meantime and wrote out all that happened, that would save a lot of time.

"Perfect," I said. "Rick has to secure this door and I can work on my statement while he makes repairs. I'll see you on Monday, Marty. Thanks for all your help. I hope I can meet Aaron Christenson sometime, too. Oh, by the way, here's this." I handed him what was left of Phil's cheap handcuffs.

Rick and I stood in the ruined doorway and watched Marty drive away. Rick turned and wrapped his arms around me.

"Oh, Maggie," he said. "I was afraid I was never going to see you again."

"I know, I know," I whispered. "I was afraid I was never going to see me, or you, or anybody, again either."

We clung to each other for a few minutes. I never felt more glad to be alive. Finally, Rick stepped back. "I want to go home and soak all of this off in the hot tub then cuddle with you," he said, "But, I have to get this door fixed. You're sure you'll be all right here by yourself?"

"Yeah, I think so, now that all of the bad guys are all rounded up. Got your phone with you? I'll call you if anything seems amiss," I said. "Now get going. The faster this door is fixed the sooner we can go home."

Rick headed to the hardware store and I sat down at my computer. Might as well get that statement done. I flexed my fingers and started to type.

CHAPTER 68

▼

By three o'clock the clinic door was fixed and Rick and I were headed home, the infamous quilt on the passenger seat of the Blazer. Rick kept his pickup nearly on my back bumper all the way, but it was nice to feel protected. In all the confusion and then with the pizza party, I had totally forgotten about the quilt. Marty would need it, I was certain. I would take it to him, but only after I figured out for sure that it had the location of the stolen money coded into it.

"This is heaven," said Rick, letting his arms float on the water in the hot tub. "I may never get out."

"You'll be boiled soon enough," I said. "You know, I forgot to give Marty that quilt."

"You'd better call him right away, Maggie. That's evidence."

"Yeah, I know. First though, I want to see if it does hold the key to the money, as Barbara had said. Besides, as long as it is in my possession the whole time the chain of evidence thing should be intact."

"How are you going to figure out what message that quilt has on it? We've gone over the thing with a fine-toothed comb already."

I shook my head. "What a dolt I am. I forgot to tell you ... now I can't even remember who it was, but one of our clients, no wait, it was Aileen, our mail carrier, who said that the French knots looked like they were arranged to form Braille words. She said her sister is blind and she learned how to read Braille when she was little and Aileen said she had learned some of it, too, at least enough to recognize it on the quilt."

"You're kidding! But, how did Barbara know Braille; she wasn't blind, was she?"

"No," I said, "But she told me during one of our conversations in the pool about her best friend from high school. That girl is blind and knew Braille. Barbara told me she had learned the basics from her. There's probably books about it, too."

"But where did she get the idea to put the code on a quilt like that?"

"Quilts have been used that way before. '"Way back during the slave years, when the Underground Railroad was functioning, there were people who were sympathetic to the slaves' plight."

Rick nodded. "Yes, of course I know about that. But, what is the connection?"

"Just this: People who were willing to help slaves escape put up signs to tell the slaves they could stop for the night, or to hide, or whatever, at those peoples' houses. The people had to be careful, though. They couldn't just hang up a "escaping slave safe house" banner, or those chasing the escaping slaves would know where to go to find them. Some people put special marks on a barn or a shed wall, others made quilts."

"And quilted the signals into the fabric; I get it." said Rick.

I nodded. "Yes. They did this a couple of ways. Some people actually stitched maps into the backs of their quilts for the escapees to use. Some made log cabin quilts, you know, that's the block that has a small center square surrounded by narrow strips of fabric, the logs, if you will. Traditionally, that center block is either yellow or red, signifying the heart or the hearth at the center of the "cabin." Log cabin quilts with a black center were a signal to an escaping slave that he was at a safe house. The people who were sympathetic to the slaves would hang the quilts out on the clothes line and the slave chasers never gave them a second glance."

"Wow. That was pretty clever. So you think that's what Barbara did?"

"That's what I'm thinking. By the way, boss, I'm taking Monday off. I want to take the quilt down to the Lilac Blind Foundation to see if it is sewn in Braille, then I need to go spend some time at the Sheriff's office."

"That'll be fine and you're right, I'm boiled. Let's go in."

CHAPTER 69

▼

Monday morning came all too soon. But at least I had gotten some sleep and I wasn't quite as sore and achy as I had been. I hoped Phil's shoulder wound was giving him all sorts of grief.

"Henry, you want to go along with me today?"

"Meow," he said, and bobbed his head yes. I couldn't really take this as a true response to my verbal question, though, as the sight of the cat carrier always gets him talking and bobbing his head. He hopped into his private transport and we took off.

"Yes," said Emily at the Lilac Blind Foundation. "This looks like Braille. Let me make a couple of calls; I should be able find someone who can read this for you."

Within minutes I was headed toward Steve Petersen's front door, Henry straining on his leash. I had asked Mr. Petersen if Henry would be a problem and he said no, bring him along. So, here we were.

"You must be Maggie." Steven Petersen opened his front door and motioned me in. "And you have your cat with you?"

"Yes, Henry loves to travel about and meet new people. He loves everybody."

Once inside, Mr. Petersen leaned over and said, "Here, kitty, kitty." Henry walked up and put his head under Mr. Petersen's hand. "How soft he is," he said.

"You can pick him up if you like," I said, "But, I have to warn you; he will hug you around the neck and probably try to lick your ear."

True to my prediction, the minute Steve Petersen picked Henry up, Henry's black nose went right into his ear. I could hear the purring and see Henry's paws flexing in delight, white claws flashing in and out of the black fur. Mr. Petersen felt his way over to what was obviously his favorite chair and sat down. He was beaming. Henry had made another friend.

Henry finally had enough of Mr. Petersen's ear and hopped down to explore.

"So, you have something for me to read for you?"

"Yes, Mr. Petersen, if you wouldn't mind. I appreciate you doing this so early in the morning for me. I think it's Braille that is sewn using French knots into a small quilt."

"Please call me Steve," he said. "Now tell me, how in the heck did Braille end up on a quilt?"

While Henry poked about, I told Steve the long story of Barbara, Phil and his posse of bad guys, and the quilt. When I was finished I handed him the quilt.

"It has a lot of lumpy seams on it," I said, "But the knots seem to be in fairly orderly rows."

"That's okay, I can manage. What a great story, though. I love mysteries and police procedurals; your story sounds like one from the books I like to read. Now, let's see about his quilt."

I watched Steve fingers run delicately across the knots on Barbara's quilt. "It says the same thing over and over," he said. "Washington Mutual, Valley Branch, box 104."

Jackpot! I thought.

"Was that what you hoped for?" he asked.

I forgot he wouldn't be able to see my smile of glee.

"Yes, that's it. That's where Phil hid his stolen money."

"Now what are you going to do?"

Steve was looking very serious. Did he think I was going to go get the money for myself?

"Take the info to the sheriff," I said. "I wouldn't touch Phil's stolen money."

Steve's face relaxed. "I'm glad to hear that," he said. "Now, how about some tea?"

CHAPTER 70

▼

With a stenographer taking down every word, I gave Marty my statement. My written out version turned out to be very helpful—I was astonished about the details that were already getting fuzzy. Hopefully I could put all this out of the front part of my brain pretty soon. I knew I'd never forget it totally, but I also didn't need to remember all the fear and discomfort so clearly. When I was done Marty and I went to the deputy's lounge for coffee.

"Thanks for the information you got off the quilt, Maggie, but when we were able to sit down and talk to Stub, stoolie that he is, spilled his guts. We actually have already recovered the money."

"Rats, here I thought I could really impress you," I said.

"Are you kidding? You have impressed this whole office," Marty said. "Just surviving the stuff that Phil put you through, rescuing Sully, all of it."

Through the lounge doorway I could see Henry sitting on Marty's desk, reveling in the petting he was getting from the other people in the office who gathered around him. "He gets some of the credit, though," I said, pointing at him. "He kept rubbing his face on the knots on that quilt. He was doing that in the clinic and that's what made our mail carrier take a closer look at the quilt than she probably would have. Otherwise, we would never have figured out that Braille."

"And now he doesn't care at all about it," said Marty. The quilt was folded up on the edge of the desk and Henry hadn't even given it a second glance.

"Yeah, I noticed that. Maybe he thinks he 'told' us what we needed to do. It's hard to give him all that credit, but it does make you wonder."

"Do you want the quilt back?" Marty asked.

"You don't have to keep it; it's not evidence?"

Marty shook his head. "No, not really. Since Stub gave us the information from the note Barbara wrote, the quilt is not important."

I shivered. I wasn't sure I wanted the thing around. But … I thought for a minute. "Okay, I'll take it. I know what I want to do with it."

Marty slid the quilt into a bag and handed it to me. "Here you go. That's about it, Maggie. I have your statement and there shouldn't be anything else until this comes to trial."

"So, Phil's going to try and plead innocent again, huh?"

"I don't know yet for sure," Marty said. "There're going to be all sorts of hoops to jump through, first. There's no way he will get off, though. There was so much forensic evidence recovered, both at Sam Hughes' house and in the little shack where he had you, not to mention what we found in the storage shed behind Valley Bowl, that a jury of six-year-olds would vote to convict him with no question of reasonable doubt. Whatever happens, he will be in prison for a long time, probably even for life without a chance for parole."

"That's good to know, Marty. I just wish I knew what made him go off the deep end like he did. We had started what seemed to be a such a good life. Well, you can't change the past, I guess. I better get out of your way; I know you have work to do. You'll have to come over for dinner one night soon."

"Thanks, Maggie, I'd like that. Keep in touch."

I hoisted Henry onto my shoulder and we headed home.

CHAPTER 71

▼

Home never looked better to me. I made a cup of coffee with a hefty slug of Kahlua in it and settled down in front of the fireplace. I was really glad I put the gas logs in, just a click of a switch and I had flames to watch and warm me up.

I sat for over an hour, just watching the fire. When my stomach started to growl I got up to find something for lunch. On my way to the kitchen I glanced out the front window and saw Georgia's Subaru SUV pull around the back and go into the garage. When she started across the lawn I opened the back door and hollered.

"Come on in and have some lunch," I said.

"Here," she said, handing me a bag of groceries. She went back to her car for two more bulging bags and we went into the kitchen with them. "I decided I needed to do some cooking. It's going to be Italian night tomorrow."

"Looks like you have enough to feed an army here, girl. What prompted this?"

"Well, I feel like I should do something to pay my way here and cooking I can do. Besides, I just got back from the lawyer's office; I just signed the last of the divorce papers."

We put away the groceries then sat down to eat. Georgia had made biscotti the day before and we crunched our way through double chocolate chip heaven that we dipped in steaming coffee.

"Good for you. It was tough to do, though, wasn't it," I said, wiping chocolate crumbs off my face with a sigh of pleasure. Nothing quite like chocolate!

"Yeah, it was a little bit. But, Ron has been giving me such a bad time for so long that it was more of a relief. Maybe I can get a life back, maybe meet somebody new, who knows?"

"Do you think Ron will fight it?"

"I don't really know for sure what he will do. He saw me as his property and may think that is true no matter what. Or, he will just fold his tent and go away; I don't know. I didn't ask for much, just what was mine when we got married, enough money to hold me over for a few months until I can find a place to live, and half the money he gets if he sells the house, seeings as how I put up all of the down payment."

"That seems awfully generous of you, Georgia. Are you sure you will be okay?"

"Oh, sure. I shouldn't have too much trouble finding another job if I decide I don't want to stay with Dr. Bryant. I worked for years as a dental assistant, you know, and I can go back to that pretty easily, I think. It seems there is always a need, if not in an actual dental office then at Spokane Community College helping to teach their program. I did that for a few semesters and they told me to call them if I ever wanted to get into the teaching end of dental assisting again. I'll just have to see. I can always get a station in a salon, too."

"That all sounds pretty reasonable. You think you will quit working at the Valley Foot and Ankle Center?"

"No, not necessarily. But, it is nice to know that I could have other options. I might actually call SCC and see if there are any classes I could teach on my days off from the foot clinic. What about you, Maggie?"

"No big changes, although I hope my life will settle down a bit now, too. Marty said Phil will be in prison for a long time; he will probably get a life sentence and never have a chance at parole. What a relief it is knowing he's back behind bars. Now, tell me what's for dinner tomorrow."

CHAPTER 72

▼

I spent Tuesday in the Killer Quilts studio, returning some semblance of order to the mess I made just days before. I popped back into the kitchen every now and then, the aroma of Italian sauces and wonderful foods drawing me like a bee to nectar. Rick came in the door with his nose in the air, too.

"What smells so wonderful?" he asked, as he hugged me hello.

"Georgia's doing Italian for us," I said. "I can hardly wait to have some."

"Me too. I'll go change. Maybe she would like me to fix us a little pre-dinner cocktail to go with her feast. Oh, and I ran into Marty at the store. He looked a bit lost and hungry, so I invited him for dinner. Maybe he could smell the pasta sauce clear over there!"

"Oh, good. I'm glad you did that. I told him just yesterday we needed to get together. This'll be perfect. Especially since my original plan for food tonight wouldn't have fed three of us very well and Georgia certainly has plenty.

"I went in and did my report today and Marty gave me back that awful little quilt that has caused so much trouble. I don't want to keep it, but I want you to do something with it for me, okay?"

"Sure," Rick said, "Whatever you need."

"Thank you for indulging me. I'll tell you about it later. Let's go get those drinks."

I turned off the lights and went through the secret door into the kitchen. "There's going to be one more mouth for dinner, Geo, that okay?"

She laughed, pointing at all the steaming and bubbling pots. "I think I can manage another plate out of this."

Georgia was a consummate Italian cook and we all ate until we were stuffed. Marty was more relaxed than I had ever seen him. As Georgia and I filled the dishwasher he even came into the kitchen to help finish with the cleaning up and he and Georgia talked like they had known each other forever. Feeling like a fifth wheel, I went back to join Rick in front of the fire.

"I think Marty has his eye on your friend," Rick whispered.

"What?" I said. I straightened up and peered toward the kitchen. "You think so? That really would be nice, Marty is lonely and Geo has had such a bad time. They could be good for each other. It's just so soon for Georgia, though, she just signed her divorce papers yesterday."

"But, how long has it been since she has had a nice guy in her life?" Rick asked. "At least we know Marty and know that he is genuine."

"That's true. Hmmmmm, Georgia and Marty. I wonder ..."

EPILOGUE

▼

Rick Evans walked across the cemetery until he found Barbara Hughes' grave. He laid a single rose across the stone marker.

"Maggie wanted you to know that Phil is in prison, probably for the rest of his life, Barbara." he said. "She also wanted you to have this."

Rick opened a small box. Inside were the ashes from the crazy quilt with the message on it that she had made. Using a small trowel, Rick worked the ashes into the dirt by the marker.

"Now you may truly rest in peace, Barbara. Maggie knew you would like to get even with Phil after what he did to you. Thanks to the quilt you made, you did. Phil committed enough crimes trying to get a hold of it to put him away for a long time."

The day had started out overcast and windy. As Rick stepped away from the grave the clouds parted, pouring beams of sun onto the ground and bathing the cemetery in a golden glow.

The End

Butterscotch Drop Cookies

t = teaspoon T = tablespoon c = cup

Use a large saucepan and you won't have to dirty a bowl:

In the pan melt ½ c of margarine or butter (1 cube)

Take the pan off the heat and mix in:

2/3 c packed golden brown sugar

1 large egg

¾ t vanilla extract, do not use imitation vanilla!

Mix the above together and add:

1 1/3 c flour combined with ¾ t baking soda

Add 1/3 c chopped nuts, pecans are the best choice, but walnuts are good too, if desired.

Put a lid on the pan and chill the dough at least for an hour until it is easy to handle. Preheat the oven to 375 degrees. Roll 1 tablespoon at a time of dough into balls and place 2 inches apart on non-greased cookie sheet. Flatten each ball slightly. You may press a half of a nut onto each cookie ball before baking, if desired. Bake for about 8 minutes. Don't let them get too done, as this should be a chewy versus a crisp cookie. The recipe makes about 2 ½ dozen.

Spicy Shrimp Florentine

This will serve two people as a main course, or four as a side dish

1 lb cooked or raw shrimp, peeled

2 green onions, chopped, white and green part or 2 T chopped raw onion

about 2 T Extra Virgin Olive Oil or any cooking oil

1 T hot chili sauce (the brand I use is called Sriracha HOT Chili Sauce, there is a rooster on the front of the bottle)

2 T oyster flavored sauce

Cook the onion in the oil just until it is soft, do not let the onion brown. Add the shrimp. Cook raw shrimp until they are pink, opaque, and have curled up, if using cooked shrimp just let them get warm.

As soon as the shrimp are ready turn off the heat.

Stir in the chili sauce and the oyster sauce. Immediately serve over a bed of rice, pasta, or cooked spinach, frozen cut leaf spinach or fresh is the best, canned spinach is too salty for this dish. Garnish with sliced hard-cooked eggs, if desired. If serving over rice or pasta, the spinach makes a nice side dish.

Oyster sauce and hot chili sauce can be found in the Asian section of most grocery stores or at an Asian market.

If you would like an illustrated copy of the instructions for the quilt Maggie makes in this book, please email me at KillerQuilts@aol.com for details.

For a sneak peak at The Workout Cat, turn the page!

I know when the screaming started that things will not be going well at the pool today. I thought about it for a minute, did I really want to go out there or should I just slip away?

I sighed. I am never smart enough to jump away from trouble and instead jump toward it. I clicked my lock shut and walked out to the pool deck.

Donna, our water aerobics instructor and one of the other class members are struggling to pull a man out of the water. He appears to be unconscious, and there is nothing heavier than dead weight like this. Arms and legs seem to develop several new joints and become about as easy to handle as cooked spaghetti.

"Somebody call 911," I yell. I threw my towel on a chair and jumped into the water to help.

Between the three of us we are finally able to drag the man up onto the edge of the pool. His face is an awful mottled blue color and his eyes are half open, unseeing, pupils dilated to a fathomless black. Donna helped me turn him onto his back and I lift his chin up and lean down to see if he was breathing. I realize as he flops over that this is LeRoy Higgins, one of my favorite people here at Stroh's Super Sportz Club.

LeRoy is not breathing and I gave him two quick breaths of air. I see his chest rise and fall, so I knew I was blowing into his lungs and not into his stomach. I slid my hand down and felt in the side of his neck for carotid pulse. No pulse, so now CPR is next.

"Anybody want to help me?" I yell as I start chest compressions. "Anybody know CPR?"

"I do," said Donna. As I moved back up to LeRoy's face to give him another two breaths she took over with compressions.

"Oh, my God, look at that!" said a panic-stricken voice. I take a quick glance as Donna does the compression part of the resuscitation we are attempting and see a trail of dark red blood flowing across the exposed aggregate surface of the pool deck and into the water, making a pink cloud. I notice every time Donna gives a chest compression the flow of blood increases. LeRoy is wounded somewhere and our CPR is not circulating the blood like we hoped, but rather helping to pump it out.

I give two more breaths and before Donna can restart compressions the pool area is full of EMTs and firemen.

Donna and I are happy to step away and let them work. Within seconds they slide a tube down LeRoy's throat and are delivering oxygen to him with an ambu bag. IVs are running wide open and LeRoy is loaded on a gurney and whisked away.

I stagger over to a chair and sit down. LeRoy was dead before we even pulled him out of the water, I know. I had seen the purple lividity. I had looked into his eyes. He is gone. I close my eyes for a minute and listen to the sounds of hysteria babbling all around me. When it suddenly got quiet I know why. The police are here.

The Workout Cat will be coming soon ... watch for it!

978-0-595-48215-3
0-595-48215-5

Printed in the United States
101123LV00004B/83/A

9 780595 482153